CURSE CORVUS

ALEX EBENSTEIN

CURSE CORVUS

© 2023 by Alex Ebenstein

Cover art by Evangeline Gallagher
Interior illustrations by Christopher Castillo Díaz
Cover & interior design by Dreadful Designs
Edited by Alex Woodroe

alexebenstein.com

First Edition: April 2023
Dreadful Books by Alex Ebenstein

ISBN: 978-1-7379740-6-2 / Paperback Edition
ISBN: 978-1-7379740-7-9/ eBook Edition

PRAISE FOR "CURSE CORVUS"

"A disturbing exploration of how far we'll go for happiness, complete with dead birds and a very toxic friendship, *Curse Corvus* will make you squeamish, haunt your nightmares, and break your heart all at once. Alex Ebenstein is most definitely a rising voice in the horror genre, and this novella proves why."

—Gwendolyn Kiste, Bram Stoker Award-winning author of *The Rust Maidens* and *Reluctant Mortals*

"Alex Ebenstein's *Curse Corvus* expertly captures the dizzying flight of a devoted friendship beset by an insidious supernatural threat. Readers will be riveted as the unsettling events build and build to a truly crushing conclusion, but it's Ebenstein's ability to ground the horror in the realistically fraying relationship between the two strong women at its center that will haunt you."

—Gordon B. White, Shirley Jackson Award and Bram Stoker Award Finalist

"Alex Ebenstein delivers an unforgettable and perfectly chilling portent. He weaves curses and eerie found objects skillfully with real-life anxieties like toxic relationships, jealousy, and suspicion. The urgency of breaking this enigmatic curse feels equally as crucial as preserving the relationship between Lindsay and Val. More haunting discoveries mount, confounding and enthralling at every turn, fulfilling ten-fold at the end. *Curse Corvus* offers a dark and thrilling ride, rife with sinister threats and true-to-life anxieties."

—Lauren Bolger, author of *Kill Radio*

"Centered by the arresting image of a wedding dress staked and surrounded by birds, Alex Ebenstein's *Curse Corvus* is a swift and emotional exploration of the dread of friendship transforming into cruelty, happiness transforming into all of its opposites. Readers will appreciate the emotional journey and the critique of capitalism here."

—Christi Nogle, author of *The Best of Our Past, the Worst of Our Future*

"Ebenstein's mastery of pacing, his ability to maintain tension, and his fine-tuned understanding of when to build and when to unravel mystery make *Curse Corvus* a truly brilliant book. Things go from not quite right to so completely wrong seamlessly, making everything that happens feel unexpected but also inevitable. It is fun, fully absorbing, and filled with dread. Even the slowest readers will find themselves flipping the last page, shocked at how easily it all went down."

—Alexis DuBon, editor of *No Trouble at All*

CURSE CORVUS

Content warnings are available at the end of this book. Please consult this list for any particular subject matter you may be sensitive to.

For Lydia and Victoria, for letting me steal your story.

ONE

I found the first dead bird, featherless and skeletal, in the trailhead parking area.

The word embryo came to mind. Was that even correct? *Embryo*. A tiny, not fully formed bird corpse, delicately and purposefully extracted from its protective shell and placed on display on the pavement. I almost stepped on the damn thing getting out of my car.

Pale and prehistoric looking.

"Oh, God," I said, still tangled in my seatbelt. I scanned the vicinity for remnants of its shell, wanting to understand—Had it just hatched? Been dragged by an animal?—but couldn't find any.

"Lindsay? You all right?" Val asked from the passenger seat.

"Yeah, fine. Just stepped on a rock, almost fell."

It was a rare spring day in Michigan that felt more like a sneak peek at summer than a day still in winter's stranglehold—a breezy, yet sunny and warm Saturday afternoon. Val and I were out for a hike at Rosy Mound Natural Area, taking the dune trail out to Lake Michigan. Hiking was a go-to activity for us, but that time it was her idea, sparked by her "concern" for my "stress levels". Besides the fact that she was justified in her assumptions— overbearing boss, supervision of vapid college kids, and… customers—the weather was too damn nice not to go. We expected to have to jockey for position on the trail with a day like that, but the parking lot was empty.

I hadn't told Val about the bird because she was squeamish. One time she accidentally stepped on a worm and lost her shit.

But Val found the next dead bird, herself. She was walking ahead of me and saw it lying in the middle of the wood chip path; my attempt to protect her for naught.

This one was older, but not by much. It was the size of my fist, curled up so neatly, covered in black down. It looked painfully fragile, so vulnerable. I was struck by how intact and peaceful the thing looked. Like it had just dropped dead in the middle of its first flight.

"Poor thing," Val said. "I wonder what happened to it."

"Yeah, me too," I responded softly. Two dead birds out in nature was hardly a shocking experience, but this didn't *feel* normal. Like a weight pulling at the bottom of my stomach, perhaps caused by the proverbial stone used to kill the two birds.

"What kind do you think it is?"

"I don't have a clue. You?"

"A baby crow maybe?" she suggested.

I shrugged, then we moved on. The remaining stretch through the trees before we reached the dunes was uneventful. Val asked if I wanted to talk about work, and I knew she knew I didn't. Her asking was an acknowledgment of my stress and frustrations, and often that was all I needed. Because some of the shitty parts of life would never change, but at least I had Val and our hikes. I joked back that the only work-related talk I'd tolerate was either a new job or a bag of money handed over on a silver platter, the latter preferable.

The wind was calm in the dense woods, swishing playfully at our hair and jackets as we walked, but when we broke through the last line of trees out onto the exposed top of the dunes, the wind whipped at us, flinging specks of sand in our faces. It was almost enough reason to turn around, but we wanted to get down to the lake and see the big waves crashing onto the shore.

The trail turned to weathered and creaky boardwalk. Val and I walked side by side. She started on about my recent boyfriends, or lack thereof—refusing to even concede that it isn't exactly easy to bond through Tinder and drinks—and since I wasn't giving her much, the conversation turned to Bobby, the guy Val had been seeing for far too long. I pretended to listen, sparing her—for once—my usual exclamation about how much of an asshole he was. He was so much worse than *not good enough* for Val. I couldn't wait for that boyfriend experiment to end.

We passed the first lookout platform and descended to a lower boardwalk, knowing this vantage point of the dunes and distant horizon had nothing on the views farther down. The hard rubber soles of my boots smacked the wooden boards, the wide planks bouncing ever so slightly to give the impression of walking on the moon, propelling us up and forward. I had my head down, watching my feet. Left, right. And Val's. Right, left. Out of step one moment, in step the next. A sloppy metaphor for our lives together rattled in my brain.

I made it another ten feet before I realized Val's boots were no longer in my field of view.

I turned back to see Val staring across the sand and growing dune grass. Val's gaze was pointed at a distant copse of young cottonwoods, or so I thought at first, but no—directly in front of us, scattered among all that dune grass, were dozens of black—

Birds. Varying sizes, but all black. All dead, too, but offering the illusion of movement as the gusting wind battered their ruffled feathers.

"What the fuck," I said, joining Val's side.

"Look at them all, Linds," she whispered suddenly. "What happened? What could do this?"

"Beats the hell out of me. Some kind of bizarre weather phenomenon? Weird pressure system, maybe?" I suggested.

"Should we call someone?"

"I don't know. Who?"

"County Parks?"

"Nah. It's weird, sure. But they're dead birds, nothing they haven't seen before… but, uh, let's get some distance from these things. Who knows if they have a disease or some shit? We should keep going. Unless you want to turn back?"

Val shook her head. "You're right. Let's keep going."

She took one last long look at the birds before setting off. I couldn't bear it, knowing the image of all those black, feathery corpses would nag at me, and I had a feeling that cloying unease would be around for a while.

We continued along the boardwalk to our destination—a perfectly placed observation deck. From there, a swath of sand backed by the full spectrum of freshwater colors—cerulean to indigo—stretching into the horizon, the starkly contrasted beige dunes crowding in on either side. Val and I had been there many times before, but it never failed to calm whatever troubled my nerves. The beauty of this moment made me happy, but it was tainted. I couldn't shake the disturbing images left in my mind by the bird carnage.

After we had our fill of nature-watching, I made the decision to take the branch trail back to the other trailhead parking lot. It would take longer to get back to the car, and we'd have to hoof it along a stretch of busy road to get to where we'd parked, but I couldn't bring myself to walk past the birds again. Val agreed.

As we made the turn on the boardwalk that set us heading east again, our pace quickened. It wasn't uncommon for us to make the return trip more quickly, having accomplished the main objective of our hike. Knowing the walk back was longer this time certainly factored into the equation, too. But it was more than that. The wind coming freely across the lake pushed at our backs, impelling us along, as if encouraging us to proceed, to discover what lay ahead.

We both noticed it at the same time. It was hard not to, really. Twenty or thirty yards in front of us, just off the side of the boardwalk, was a wedding dress. It hung over the post of a trail marker like it would on a mannequin at a bridal shop, lacy sleeves flapping furiously in the breeze.

"You're seeing that, too, right?" Val asked. "Not just me?"

"Yeah."

"This day just keeps getting weirder, doesn't it?"

"Yeah," I said again, noticing we'd both slowed. We were still moving toward it, but warily, as if coming up on the dress too fast would draw danger to ourselves.

The dress was slightly off-white in color, whether from age or by design, I couldn't tell. The style was similar to what my mother wore on her wedding day. *So* much lace. Although I only ever saw it once—right before Mom set fire to it after my deadbeat drunk of a father abandoned us—I remembered it well. Thank God I'd never be asked to wear it someday.

For a second, the wind hit the dress in such a way that it filled out, sleeves and all, as if there was suddenly an invisible person inhabiting it—not a wooden post. And in that moment, I could almost see her, the one who left this dress behind. A young woman, plain of features, but radiant when a rare smile parted her lips… purchased the second-hand dress, possibly due to lack of money, but more likely in rebellion against the outrageous cost of a new, designer dress… yet despite that, despite rejecting society's standards of beauty, wondered if this dress was enough to make her beautiful, make her special.

That thought led to the next, obvious thought: why was the dress left there? Was the bride abandoned on her wedding day? Or grieving the end of her marriage? Celebrating?

In the span of a couple seconds, I had created an entire imaginary person, played out various scenarios to their life, felt complex emotions regarding each path. I knew it was all pointless. Still, the visual of this wedding dress out in the dunes and the sheer absurdity of the matter felt so evocative to me, I couldn't help but wonder where it came from.

Then I noticed the dress wasn't alone.

"What do you think that is at the base there?" I asked Val, pointing to a swaddled bundle of what looked like old floral-patterned bedsheets tied together with a length of lace ribbon. The bundle was a couple feet long and nestled up against the four by four post the dress hung from.

"I'm not sure I want to know," Val said, yet she kept going. Closer and closer.

My imaginary character forgotten, I suddenly had a feeling that we'd just walked into...*something*. I wanted to believe it was something lighthearted. Like maybe this was a proposal? Or we were about to be on the receiving end of a weird, stupid practical joke? I could have believed either—or neither—and had to fight the opposing urges of wanting to run away before we ruined someone's surprise and spinning around with my arms splayed, shouting "Good one! You got us! Ha ha!"

I could tell, even in my own thoughts, how impulsive and overexcited those reactions would be, and I think that spoke to the nature of what I was really feeling. That the *something* we stumbled upon was something we shouldn't be seeing. It wasn't meant for us. Or worse, it *was* meant for us, and we wouldn't want any part of it. A proposal or joke was too easy, too convenient. The wedding dress and whatever lay bundled below were bad news. That dune of dead birds wasn't looking so bad anymore.

An image of a dead baby flashed through my mind. Discarded, bloated, wrapped in a shroud beneath the gown of my imaginary, abandoned bride...

Val bent to the bundle. She pulled the end of the bow, careful to leave everything else in place.

"Wait—"

Val drew back the top flap, screamed, and fell backwards.

TWO

I rushed to Val.

She held her arm out to stop me, as if to protect me from whatever she uncovered. She was too late. I already saw what lay within the sheets, and I couldn't prevent the yelp from exiting my mouth.

A bird. Another fucking bird.

Although mostly covered, what I could see was all black. The beak, the sleek, shiny feathers. A crow, I assumed. Yet I couldn't remember ever seeing one so big.

"Raven," Val said, still seated on the sand, staring at the bird bundle propped against the post.

"Is that what it is?" I asked, crouching beside her. "I was thinking crow. What's the difference?"

"I'm not sure there is one, except maybe size. And this bird *is* big, isn't it?"

"Biggest I've ever seen up close."

My hand reached out, as if it had a mind of its own, longing to touch the bundle and the bird inside. At the very least, hoping to pull back the sheet more and see if there was any truth left to reveal. My fingers made it within an inch when Val's hand stopped them short. We stayed that way for a few seconds, frozen. Val watching me watching the dead bird.

The bird's eye moved.

I yelled and snatched my hand back, flinging Val's away in the process. She made a surprised and confused noise while my breath stopped in my throat and I faltered back. Yet I continued to stare and stare and…

The bird was dead. The eye didn't move. Couldn't have moved.

The black, soulless pupil was clouded over with the wispy, murky gray of death. Staring back at me, yes, but unmoving.

Val was saying something.

"Huh? What?" I said, looking at her finally.

"What was that? Are you okay? You're not hurt, are you?" She was always asking me that. Always worried about me.

"Yeah, I'm fine. No need for twenty questions. I just…I don't know. I thought the bird moved."

She glanced quickly at the raven or crow or whatever damned kind of bird it was, then back at me, questioning. "…it didn't, though. Did it?"

I tried to laugh it off, but it sounded too forced, and hollow. "Of course not. I spooked myself, is all. Let it get to me, I guess."

"You're not the only one," Val said, giving her head a quick shake. "This is fucking weird."

And I knew how much she meant it, because Val never swore. Like, ever. Saying it now sounded so unnatural, so unlike her that for a second, I forgot myself and nearly laughed out loud. But I bit it back in time, which was good, because I would have hurt her feelings, and she didn't deserve that, least of all for being honest and open. Not that she would have said as much, but I would have known.

"Yeah, I don't know what's going on here, but I don't like it. Let's get going."

I held a hand out to Val to help her up, but she didn't take the offer. She was rubbing the fingers on her right hand, as though trying to ease pain.

"Are you okay?"

"Huh?" She looked at me, then seemed to notice for the first time what she was doing with her hands, and quickly dropped them to her side. "Oh, yeah, I'm fine. Must have landed awkwardly on my hand. No biggie."

She stood without my help and dusted off her pants.

I pulled my jacket tighter around me, feeling chilled despite the sun. Even the wind had lulled for the time being, letting the dress fall slack. It seemed the cold lived within, not without. I officially had enough of whatever bullshit we'd stumbled upon.

"Ready Val?" I asked, already moving away from the scene.

"Wait."

I looked over my shoulder at her but couldn't convince myself to fully turn back.

"We have to call someone *now*, right?"

I shrugged. "If you want, sure. I just want to go."

Val looked between me and what I was beginning to think of as a ritualistic site. I could see her debating internally. She was probably right. This shit was beyond weird enough to warrant a call. But to who? Police? Parks maintenance? Sure, yeah, maybe. But what would they do? Clean it up? We could do the same. Except right then I was tired, over it. I wanted to be gone minutes ago, and I desperately hoped she wouldn't ask me to stay because I knew I couldn't say no.

Either Val sensed my feelings or came to the same conclusion because she nodded. "Fine."

She bent once more to the bundle, did something I couldn't see, then straightened, smoothed her jacket, and joined me on the boardwalk.

"What were you doing?"

"Felt like I needed to cover it back up, you know?"

"I suppose so," I responded, but my mind was barely there. I was already doing mental exercises to block the images from the past hour, already focusing solely on getting back to the car.

Whether picking up whatever brain waves I was transmitting, or feeling the same sort of unease, Val remained quiet the rest of the way out.

Neither of us talked, but my thoughts chattered continuously. On the walk, on the drive, all day and night. By attempting to block the images, I only succeeded in forcing my brain to continually confront the very things I was trying to get out of my head.

A part of me knew I was overreacting. I had to be. Right?

Well, I *wanted* to be. The bird, the dress… A practical joke was all that was, or an attempt at romance that went over our heads. Nothing more.

That was what I told myself, over and over and over…

So why did I feel like it was far from over?

THREE

Eventually I was able to stop thinking about the bird— and all the other birds, a hundred or more of them— and the dress. It took all of that Saturday night, but I was able to fall asleep only a little later than normal, just after midnight.

The reprieve did not last long, however.

Because I couldn't let it go. I couldn't chalk it up to a weird happenstance and move about my day, because that wasn't me. I did not let things go.

So, I did some research. Which meant the next time I met up with Val—for happy hour drinks at Grand Bar a couple days later—I was armed with an answer.

Well, a partial answer, anyway.

"Bird kill," I blurted as soon as the bartender left to pour our beers, a little louder than I intended. A loner guy down the bar eyed me curiously, but a quick furrow of my eyebrows had him staring into his beer again.

"I'm sorry, what?" Val said.

"It's a thing," I said, turning to face her. "2011 in Sweden, about a hundred jackdaws—those are similar to crows, but in Europe, I think. Oh, and get this. In Arkansas, in both 2010 *and* 2011, literally *hundreds* of blackbirds. And then in—"

"Whoa, whoa, whoa! Linds, slow down. What are you talking about?"

I stared at her like *she* was the one acting crazy.

"The other day? The birds?"

"Yeah...? What about them?"

"Well," I said, drawing the word out obnoxiously. "I've been thinking about everything we saw, and I figured there *had* to be an explanation for it all. You know, scientifically?"

"Sure," she said, as the bartender returned with our beers. She lifted her mug to me and I tapped it with mine, then we both tapped them onto the bar top before taking a long, deep first drink—standard protocol.

"Okay, so, I guess 'scientifically' is the wrong word because scientists don't exactly always have an explanation or cause, but 'bird kill' *is* a thing. It's apparently a localized event that results in a large number of bird deaths. You know, like what we saw the other day."

"You think that's what it was?" she said.

"Why not? I guess it's not *exactly* an answer, since the phenomenon is relatively unexplained, but it inherently puts the blame on *something*. You know, like disease or weather or whatever? It has to be this, because if not, then what? You know? What could have caused that many birds to die?"

I'd been talking too much, too fast. I took a drink to slow me down, calm me down. Val had been nodding her head along with my frantic words, but I could tell something was on her mind.

"What about the dress and the raven, then?"

She asked it so matter-of-fact-ly, so *I see what you're saying, but what about this?* that I wanted to scream. *Of course* I hadn't forgotten about the dress and the bundle. How could I? But I needed to lean on *something*, for God's sake, and bird kill, while just a term I found on the internet, was exactly that. A form of explanation. And, frankly, the current savior of my sanity. My mind could handle dismissing one bizarre thing or the other, but not both.

Val just didn't seem interested in my explanation.

"Probably a prank or something," I said. "Or, I don't know, art school students with too much time and too many drugs. They saw the birds before us and decided to do a little *artistic expression*." I didn't really believe that, but I didn't want to dwell on it either. I couldn't dwell on it.

"I don't know," she said, fingering the rim of her glass. Her brown eyes were unfocused, staring at the shelves of liquor bottles across the bar top.

"You don't know what?"

"Drugged out art students," she said, shaking her head slowly.

I didn't respond. I watched her until she finally looked my way. Her expression was one of impatience, seeming to ask me: *What? What are you looking at me like that for?*

I grunted, annoyed and unsure of why she was being weird about it. "Care to elaborate, o wise one?"

"Obviously they were left behind. That doesn't happen by accident. But I don't believe they were left behind by your druggy art kids."

"Oh, you don't, do you," I interrupted, sarcastically.

She ignored me. "See, I've been thinking about it quite a bit the past couple days, too, and while I can't explain it, I...Well, I get the feeling that there's more to it than that. It felt *more* intentional than some bored teens. You know? It felt like we walked up on the site of an ancient ritual."

I had been taking a drink when she said that last bit and choked on my beer, coughing to clear my throat. *Ritual.* That was the word in my mind, too. So now I knew she was thinking the same thing. We hadn't said a word about any of it since leaving the site, yet we both thought the same thing. I was relieved to have my best friend share these thoughts, but also scared to have encouragement to think these things.

"Yeah..." I finally admitted. "I had the same thought. But what kind of ritual? It's basically a joke still, right? Like, you can kill as many ravens as you like, but that doesn't mean anything will happen."

"Right, yeah. Of course not. Whoever left it might have thought they were being serious, but it's not *real*."

"No, not real," I agreed, taking another drink.

We lapsed into silence for a few minutes until the bartender came back. He startled us when he asked if we wanted another round. Both of us were lost in thought, I guess. I checked Val to get an indication of where she was at. She was usually good for at least a couple, and I knew she didn't have much going on after. Same with me.

Val nodded, nearly imperceptibly, but I knew the motion well.

"Yeah, we'll take another," I said.

The bartender brought us the next round and quickly left to tend to the random loners scattered down the bar. I didn't know this guy super well, but I did know he was normally more conversational. For that matter, so were we. He must have felt the vibe in our little pair and sensed that we weren't up for any flirtatious banter. It was too bad, really, because he was one of the hotter ones. Any other day and I would have been working my game. I was in a bit of a rut, and I could have used some validation. Or a distraction.

"So, let's play a game," I said, trying to keep my tone casual. "Let's say, just for fun, that this ritual, or whatever, actually *was* real. Like, whatever the person or people intended to happen actually *did* happen… What do you think it would be?"

"A curse," Val said quickly, nodding to herself. "Or maybe a *gift*. Yeah."

"Why do you say that?"

"Oh, I don't know, seems like something a witch might do." Her lips twitched into a half smile. "If witches and the occult were real, of course."

Then she laughed, but the laugh sounded all wrong. Forced, uneasy, I wasn't sure exactly, but I winced at the sound of it before hastening to cover up my reaction.

"You good, Val?" I asked, because I couldn't leave it alone.

Val nodded again. "Sure, I'm good. A bit tired, I guess."

"Haven't been sleeping well?"

"Nah. Not well at all." She took a slug from her beer, then pushed the half empty glass away from her. "If you don't mind, I think I'm going to head out. I have a couple things I need to get done and I want to get to bed early tonight."

She stood, smacking a ten and a five on the bar in front of where she had been sitting. "You can finish that if you want," she said, pointing at her beer.

Since we'd met in the freshman dorms at college, I'd never seen her leave a beer unfinished.

FOUR

I didn't see Val again for a week. That might not seem crazy for most folks and their best friends, but for us that was as unlikely as…well, as finding a hundred dead birds—an occurrence local news stations latched onto for a solid hour before the internet provided a better, more divisive story.

We texted the usual amount in the couple days after happy hour, but I could tell something was still off. Not *way* off, but response times were longer, responses shorter. More than that though, her texts felt like she was trying too hard to say what she thought I wanted to hear. What she thought she was supposed to say. Sure, I could have been overthinking, over-analyzing everything, but I knew I wasn't. After probably millions of texts between us over the years, I could tell when something was wrong.

Then Val went radio silent for a few days.

I texted, called, hit her up through socials, and got nothing in return. A mutual friend of ours, Sarah, worked with her at the University Admissions office, so I reached out to her, too. Sarah said Val had been out for a few days, called in sick. Of course, then I was really freaked out. This was so not even remotely like her. Worry ate at me from the inside, ruining my sleep and the ability to perform my own job well—not that I was saving lives or anything, just managing a clothing store—but I knew my boss noticed, and that bitch wasn't keen on the idea of mental health days.

I assumed the absolute worst had happened to Val, as only I know how to do, coming up with a litany of awful outcomes that ranged from unlikely—slipped in the shower and hit her head and died—to downright impossible—stalked by a serial killer and murdered.

But then...then I settled on a scenario that not only seemed possible, but probable.

That son of a bitch Bobby Hayes.

I started thinking back to her odd texts—how they seemed off, out of order, and how maybe it wasn't that *Val* was texting me weirdly, but her overbearing boyfriend Bobby. Maybe, just maybe, he'd done something to her, and he was the one texting me from Val's phone. I didn't know for sure if Bobby had ever been physically abusive, but I knew he was verbally and emotionally abusive.

I'd seen it firsthand on the day Val introduced us. We were at a party and she got up for a second helping of food, and Bobby made a cruel remark about her gaining weight. He laughed at the end so people would *know he was joking*, but there was no denying the sincerity in his comment. And there was no denying the hurt that clouded over Val's eyes before she steeled herself and threw her plate away instead of refilling it.

Now, there was no room for that kind of bullshit anywhere, anytime, but at that point Bobby was so new—they'd only been on three dates—so I lost my damn mind. I called him out in front of everybody, told him he better apologize and *beg* Val for forgiveness. Bobby became indignant. Val became embarrassed. They both basically told me to shut up. Bobby reiterated that it was *just a joke*, but I saw the look in his eyes. It matched the words he whispered into my ear later that night when no one else was around: *Fuck you. Don't mess with me.*

I replied, *Same to you, pal,* and walked away. I wasn't going to let him intimidate me. I always had some form of weapon and pepper spray on me. I'd also spent years taking self-defense classes. Perks of being a woman, I guess. If the fucker wanted to come at me, I was going to do whatever was in my power to drag his sorry ass to hell.

I never could understand why she stuck with him, the obvious jackass and abuser that he was. I still didn't. If I wanted to play pop-psychologist, I could guess it had something to do with her relationship with her dad. And mom, for that matter. But that was a cheap assessment, and there were more psychological factors involved that were far above my intellect. Which was why, no matter what I said, no matter how many times I promised I would keep her safe, Val would look at me sadly, tell me she loved him, and that I had nothing to worry about. Of course I knew it wasn't nothing, but the looks she'd give me said the locks were thrown on the doors of her emotions, and there was no point in me continuing to knock.

Without a doubt, if there was ever an abuser, it was Bobby Hayes, and I figured it was only a matter of time before that abuse became physical, if it hadn't already. So not hearing from Val in days had me worried that time had come.

I sent out a final round of communication—texts, voicemails, social media—letting her know I was coming over to check on her, then drove to her apartment building. I buzzed her apartment as a formality, certain I would have to wait for someone to come down and let me in and then go bang on Val's door until she—or Bobby—opened the door.

Except Val's voice popped over the intercom, grainy and electronic, like a robotic bee, asking who was there.

"Val? It's Lindsay."

"Oh hey, Linds. Come on up."

I ascended the two flights of stairs to her third-floor apartment and found her door propped open by the deadbolt. I let myself in.

Patch, Val's fat calico cat—officially named Mr. Pumpkin Patch because his mostly round orange splotches of fur looked like pumpkins against the rest of his dark, dirt-colored fur—greeted me first, purring and rubbing against my legs. I didn't know why, but that furry dude loved me. I liked animals for the most part, but they didn't seem to return the feeling. But Patch, an otherwise surly, standoffish cat—even to Val—was the extreme exception.

Val was in the kitchen, watching me as I closed the door.

"Hey Linds, how's it going? Want a beer?"

"What the—Yeah, sure, I'll take a beer. But what the hell, Val?"

Val took her time, popped the top and walked it to where I stood by her small, round dining table, only a couple steps from the door. She gave me a smile and passed the beer, as if she was doing the most normal, typical thing in all the world.

Any other time it would have been.

"I repeat: what the hell?"

"What?"

"Where have you been? I've been trying to get a hold of you for days."

"Oh, yeah, that. I had the flu. Or something, I don't know."

"The flu? Where's Bobby?"

"Bobby? I'm guessing work. Since when do you care where Bobby is?" She asked it lightly, almost like teasing.

"Has he been staying here with you?"

"Well, he *was*, but not in several days. I told him to stay at his place since I was sick."

"Right, the flu. So you said."

"Yep, or another virus. I was down and out for a few days. Felt like I was dying." Val shrugged as if it were inconsequential. "Lindsay, what is going on? You're acting like I did something wrong here."

My throat issued an involuntary noise—a mix between a laugh, a scoff, and a disgusted grunt. I had no clue what I expected to find when I got to Val's, but it sure as hell was not this.

"Me?" I asked, too loud for the close apartment quarters. Patch, who was still lingering by my feet, scurried off at the sound. "You dropped off the face of the planet for a few days, then you tell me you had a severe sickness that made you feel like you were *dying*, and yet you wonder what is going on with *me*? You didn't think to reach out at all?"

I realized then that I was still standing just inside the door, Val back several feet by the kitchen, facing me. Like a standoff. I still held the beer, too, gripping it tightly. I set

27

it on the table, wanting to sit but feeling like that would come across as me giving in.

Val shrugged again. "I feel great now. Better than I have in a long time, actually. I didn't think it was worth mentioning. But—" She leaned toward me slightly, raising both hands. "I'm sorry for not reaching out."

I wanted to scream. The notion of not thinking to tell your best friend you have a multi-day, death-like sickness was absurd enough, but I wasn't even convinced she was telling the truth. My mind was stuck on Bobby having something to do with whatever *really* happened. That being said, I felt the sincerity in her apology, and couldn't come up with a reasonable response to any of it, so instead I finally sat and took a large swig of beer.

Then, in true, maddening Val fashion, she said the one thing that could possibly distract my mind enough to allow for a change of subject.

"I have an idea for a new tattoo."

FIVE

"Why the hell didn't you start with that?" I asked, grabbing my beer and moving to the armchair in the living room—which was not so much a room as a space adjacent to the designated kitchen area. Val even had the two-bed, two-bath layout, but the place was still small. She made decent money at her job, but with rent skyrocketing, there was only so much your money could afford in a rental. And her apartment was practically luxury compared to my one-bedroom.

Val went to the loveseat across from me and sat cross-legged. She was grinning; eager.

It wasn't that getting tattoos was our *thing*, because anyone who said *such and such is my thing* was secretly—or obviously—a loser. But, Val and I *did* love getting tattoos, were perhaps a bit addicted, and whenever we had money, that's where it would go.

We had the necessary cash now, but Val hadn't been able to figure out what she wanted done. I had plans for a short quote in my mom's handwriting from a letter she wrote me years ago. Val had recently finished her half-sleeve and didn't know what to do next.

"So, I was just texting Rosie—" our tattoo artist, Rosario Torres, who had become a close friend, "—a few minutes before you got here, and she has a couple back-to-back slots open Wednesday night. What do you think?"

I ignored the fact that she had texted Rosie before me because I was too excited. I'd been waiting *months* for Val to be ready to go again, because I would not break our one tattoo rule: we had to go together. We got our first tattoos together when we were eighteen, and as far as I was concerned, we were going to get our last one together, too, as badass old women.

"Well yeah, of course. You know how long I've been waiting for you. What did you decide on?"

Val smiled, sheepishly. "It's a surprise. But you'll love it, I know. It's perfect."

"Come on. You're not going to tell me?"

"Not for a few more days. I want you to see it when it's done and be surprised and love it," she said, the excitement vibrating through her words.

"Hmm. Alright. Do you still have to work on the design with Rosie?" As soon as I figured out what I was doing for my next tat, I always sent it to Rosie, so she was up to speed and ready for me.

Val held up her phone. "Just told her what I was thinking and shared an example photo. She says she knows exactly how to draw it. She's going to mock it up tonight."

"Well okay then. I guess we'll see it on Wednesday. In the flesh, so to speak," I said, winking at Val. She laughed, and it came across as an easy, effortless giggle.

She really *was* feeling good. I hadn't seen her that high-spirited in months. And I said as much. "You look so happy, Val."

"I *am* happy, Linds. I feel wonderful."

"Why the sudden change?" I asked, then added quickly, "It's great, regardless, obviously." But, frankly, I was feeling envious. I always wanted my best friend to be happy and have good things happen for her, but it'd been a rough...well, long stretch for me, and it was sort of nice to have a close friend to commiserate with.

Except now she looked like a changed woman, and I couldn't really relate. I felt momentarily alone and lost at sea while in the physical presence of the one person who had always been there for me. It was a shitty thing to think, but that was how I felt.

Val shrugged. "Perspective, I guess."

"How do you mean?"

"That flu took a lot out of me. I don't know if I actually almost died, but there were a couple times when I remember thinking that I wanted to. Pretty bleak, huh? Now that it's over, though, I feel *alive*."

I didn't know what to say. There was too much. It felt like I was talking to a stranger. What I *did* say was, "You didn't go to the doctor at all? ER? That sounds fucked up."

"I know. It's hard to explain. When I first started feeling off I thought maybe it was food poisoning. I'd had a couple chili dogs from Johnny's Dogs—you know the risk in that—so I'm thinking, not good, but nothing I can't handle. Stay hydrated and stick near my bathroom, right? I took a nap and when I woke up it was somehow seven hours later and that *off* feeling had gone from zero to one hundred. That was Wednesday into Thursday. Honestly, not really sure what happened after that until this morning. To say I was in a haze would be the understatement of the century. I must have eaten or drank water or went to the bathroom, but I don't remember doing any of those—"

"Holy shit."

"—things, and I survived."

Val held up both hands, palms up, then dropped them into her lap.

"Sarah said you called in sick?"

"Right. I don't remember doing that either, but I did. I saw that in my call history and texts. I guess at least deathly ill Val still knows how to take care of herself. *Myself.*"

She laughed. I stared.

Val's face softened, and she said, "I can see you're still worried, but don't be, really. I'm fine. No, not fine. *Excellent.* Couldn't be better. Seriously, I'm good. Can we be good? I really am sorry about not talking to you."

I leaned back, relaxed the vice grip I didn't know I had on the chair's arms. My bullshit detector was still ticking, but slower, winding down. Either she was telling the truth, or my brain wasn't allowing myself to believe she was lying, because eventually I accepted her story.

"Yeah, okay. Clearly, it's not your fault. Sounds like a hell of a bad trip. We're good," I said. "Definitely. Although...I really wish you'd tell me your tat idea!"

Val laughed again, just full of it now. "Only a few more days. The surprise will be worth it."

"Alright..." I said, pretending to pout.

"Wednesday," she said.

"Wednesday," I agreed.

SIX

I met Val downtown at Inspired Ink on Wednesday, showing up at the same time, running into each other at the door.

"Whoa, cute shirt," I said when I saw her. I meant it, but it also stopped me in my tracks. Low cut would have been an understatement. Which, hey, get on with your bad self, but a top like that was so unlike Val that if she'd told me she even owned anything like it I would have laughed in her face. She never wore clothes like that because, in her own words, she *had nothing to show off.*

I would have swapped boobs with her in a second if I could, and I knew Val would have been all in, too. She'd always wanted to fill out her tops, whereas I wanted to get away with not wearing a bra. Go figure.

Right now, though, Val looked downright sexy, and as she smiled and told me thanks I realized it wasn't just the shirt that had caused my reaction. She was radiating, exuding so much positive energy I could have sworn she was vibrating, even though all she'd done with her shoulder length hair was toss it up in a loose bun. Val was the embodiment of strength, happiness, and *take-no-shit* attitude.

All this change was a marvel to see, and that wasn't exactly fair. It wasn't unusual for both of us to show up for a new tat with a feeling of empowerment. Making an artistic, bold choice about our own bodies did that. But we always showed up with nearly equal measures of nervous, anxious energy. Excited for what we were doing, but still a little fearful that afterwards we might feel that son of a bitch *disappointment*, or worse: *regret*. That never happened for either of us before, but past experience wasn't enough to keep apprehension at bay.

Until now, apparently. When Val opened the door to the tattoo parlor and entered before me, she was full of the good with zero helpings of the bad. And for the second time in less than a week, I found myself feeling pangs of jealousy.

For once, I was coming to get new ink, a tattoo I'd had in mind for months, and none of the positive vibes were shining through. Instead, all I felt was worry. Not that it wouldn't look good—Rosie was too damn good for that to be the case—but worried the new permanent message on my arm wouldn't mean what I thought it would mean to me, plucked out of context and needled into my skin.

I knew I was being overly pessimistic, but that had been my mood for several days up to that point. Something I couldn't shake.

Val surprised me further by choosing one of the bench seats instead of following me back to Rosie's station like she always did. I made a confused, questioning face and she responded something about giving me my space. I wanted to believe it was said with sincerity and care because she knew how personal this tattoo was for me, but the tone was all wrong. Ironically, it was enough to make me okay with her staying back.

Once settled in Rosie's chair, I saw the scan of the sentence about to be inked into my skin and made a sound partway between a sigh and a gasp.

"You good?" Rosie asked, sidling up to the chair with all her supplies and equipment.

I smiled, momentarily embarrassed, and made half-hearted excuse. "Yeah, I'm good. Happy to be here after such a shitty day at work."

"You mean to tell me managing a chain clothing store isn't all it's cracked up to be?"

Coming from just about anyone else, it would have been insulting, but not Rosie. Never Rosie. I laughed, and said, "Maybe it wouldn't be so bad if my coworkers weren't a bunch of dipshit college kids and my boss wasn't such a bitch. She tried to pull some shit threatening to fire me for leaving early today. But whatever. There was no way I was missing this appointment."

"Well you know I approve. Ready to rock and roll?"

"Hell yeah, let's do it," I said, hoping the nervousness didn't come through loud and clear to her like it did to me.

With my help, Rosie fitted the stencil to the inside of my left forearm. One step closer to being real. I felt tears fighting to make its way from my eyes after the first letter was finished, but quickly swiped it away before it could become a surge. I should have known, but somehow didn't fully anticipate that night being so emotional. All my tattoos were personal with meaning, but that new one had the deepest emotional connection yet. I knew it when I had the idea in the first place, but that had been so long ago. Waiting for Val to be ready created a sort of distance, a barrier against its deep meaning. Or, I had successfully done what I always did and buried anything remotely emotional under the years of already repressed memories.

After the first word was done, Rosie stopped. "Oh shit, I totally forgot. My bad."

Before I could ask what she meant, she was up and getting music going on her Bluetooth speaker.

Pretty Hate Machine by Nine Inch Nails. Of course.

Rosie always played that album when she worked on me, because she knew how much I liked it, and she seemed to feed off the industrial vibes. She came back to the chair, grinning. I offered a smile in return, but didn't trust myself to speak. I was beginning to shatter inside.

By the end of the first song, the tears were flowing. It startled Rosie, who pulled back and asked if I was all right. I nodded through the tears, wiping them poorly with the sleeve of my free arm, then waved a hand dismissing my outburst. Without another word, Rosie resumed her work, and I loved her for it. She must have understood, to the degree that she could have, knowing the tattoo had something to do with my mom. Tears were probably nothing entirely new for her, anyway.

What Rosie didn't know, though, was that the sentence was the closing line in a letter my mom left me the night she died, five years past. A quote from Toni Morrison, written with the beautiful imperfectness of my mother's handwriting.

Something that is loved is never lost.

The other thing Rosie didn't know was that *Pretty Hate Machine* was the only album on repeat for weeks after Mom took her own life. The album that I associate with her death, but also with grief and denial and acceptance and hope.

Eventually the tears subsided, and I had enough breath to ask Rosie a question, to change the subject. "So, what's Val got planned?"

Rosie stopped in the middle of a letter, which was so unlike her. She was good at talking and inking, but she'd never stop at random. She looked at me curiously.

"You don't know?" she asked.

"No, I don't… What is it?"

I could tell immediately she felt uncomfortable, like she was being asked to do something she shouldn't but didn't know why she shouldn't.

"It's bold, I'll say that." She shook her head. "Unique, for her," she added, then suddenly her face clouded over. "Did she say it was a surprise?"

"Yeah. She said I'd love it."

Rosie's face changed. Lighter, with a resurgence of her normal amount of mania. "Well, the drawing is dope as fuck, if you don't mind me tooting my own horn." She leaned closer to me and whispered, conspiratorially, "Which I love to do," then winked.

The Rosie I knew was back. I didn't know who that other person was before, but now, bent over my arm, laser focused again, I could tell the conversation was over. I'd have to wait to see after all.

Rosie finished up ten minutes later, then it was Val's turn. She told me to wait in the front lobby to keep her tattoo a real surprise, which was fine. I didn't mind having the time to myself, to stare at my arm. I couldn't take my eyes off the words inked forever into my skin. Rosie had replicated the words and handwriting perfectly. I was so utterly in love with the result, yet the whole experience left me exhausted and bruised and wounded all over again. Reliving the memories of getting the call about my mom, of finding the letter in my old room, of reading and rereading every line through wet, blurred vision…it didn't ruin me like it once did. But those memories never ceased to pick at the scar, produce a new tendril that would need healing. I didn't think they ever would.

I waited for almost three hours, longer than I expected. We'd both had long tattoo sessions before, but with a relatively spur of the moment idea, I had assumed Val landed on something smaller, less complex. I was bent over my phone, dicking around on Twitter when she finally emerged into the lobby, so I didn't see her right away. When I looked up she was turned away, still chatting with Rosie.

"Well?" I said. "Are you going to make me wait with bated breath or what?"

Val turned to face me, at once revealing her new tattoo and explaining the unusual shirt choice.

A raven, exploding up out of her meager cleavage and across her chest.

SEVEN

"So, what do you think? You love it," Val said.

I was unaware of how long I'd been sitting there in silence, feeling a rotten snake writhe in my stomach, growing with every second I stared at Val's new tattoo. I *did*, however, notice that confidence bursting from Val again. She'd asked what I thought, but she wasn't *really* asking. She didn't ask if I loved it, she was making a statement: I loved it.

Except, not only did I *not* love her new tattoo, the fucking thing scared the hell out of me. The shimmering purple-black ink wasn't depicting any old raven. Rosie had etched *the* raven on her chest. Not a lively bird, wings spread and taking flight, but *the* raven.

Dead. Sacrificed.

The only thing missing was the sheet to bundle it up. Although, I figured if Val removed her shirt I'd see the old sheet puddled at the base of her ribs.

"Uhh, yeah. It's…wow," I finally said, just to say something, but not allowing myself to commit to the full lie Val wanted to hear. It didn't matter, though—she wasn't listening. Val was back to Rosie, gushing over the job she'd done, and hey, kudos to Rosie—she fucking nailed it.

Val continued her compliments and Rosie did her level best to both accept and deflect the praise. I stared in shock at Val, at what I could see of the tattoo. I didn't *like* what I was seeing, but I couldn't pull my eyes away. Instantly I was back to that windy day on the dune, unable to stop looking at the bundled bird under the wedding dress.

The tattoo truly was a work of art. Whether Rosie intended to or not, she managed to recreate the raven in such a way that it even seemed to move like a real raven, buffeted by the wind, except in this case moving with Val's skin, shimmering in the light of the—

The raven's eye moved.

It was watching me, following in the same way the eyes of painted portraits do.

"Whoa, Rosie. How the hell did you do that?"

"Do what?" she asked.

I pointed. "How'd you draw the eye so it looks like it's moving?"

Rosie gave me a confused look, glanced at Val's chest, then back to me. "What are you talking about?"

I took another look at the tattooed raven and saw the eye was, of course, not moving. In fact, it looked extra dead, if that were possible. Milky, filmed over.

Embarrassed, head shaking, I muttered, "Never mind. Sick work on the tat."

I started to turn, to get the process of leaving the shop underway, when I caught a smirk floating over Val's lips. No longer simple happiness or confidence, but like she'd pulled something off. It was, decidedly, like everything else that night: entirely unlike Val. That sick, twisted rot in my stomach tightened, rose up into my chest.

I swallowed, choking back the poisonous dread in my throat like vomit. I rushed to the door and said over my shoulder, "Hey, gotta run. Feeling off all of a sudden, like I'm coming down with something. I'll catch you guys later."

And I *was* feeling sick, just not the way Val and Rosie probably imagined. They both spoke at the same time, expressing words that sounded like concern, but I wasn't paying attention. I was already out the door and on my way to my car.

I drove straight home to my apartment and downed a shot of whiskey before I remembered it was a bad idea, new tattoo and all. Funny thing is, at the time I couldn't pinpoint what exactly had me so upset. Was it seeing a near perfect copy of the raven after it'd spooked me so bad more than a week earlier? Was it because the raven was now a permanent fixture on my best friend, that I'd have to look at all the time? Or could it be that I was beginning to think I didn't know my best friend as well as I thought I did?

All the above?

I slammed another shot—health risks be damned—needing the fire in my throat, needing to burn the sick feeling away and needing to smother the trembling in my limbs. I grabbed my MacBook from my room and came back to the couch. It was too early to sleep, and even if I wanted to, sleep wouldn't come.

I turned on the TV. The local news popped on—the last channel I'd watched—and the anchors were talking about a woman found washed up on a beach at Lake Michigan. Not an uncommon occurrence, although usually that sort of thing happened later in the summer when the weather was hot and people ignored red flag warnings so they could cool off in the lake. Riptides would take them under and out into the depths to drown.

Was the news ever not bleak? I didn't need more of that right now, and I didn't feel like hunting for something else to watch, so I turned the TV off. Instead, I did what I always did on sleepless nights: get lost down the rabbit holes of the world wide web. The difference this night was that instead of scrolling social media feeds and clicking links until I couldn't remember how I'd gotten to a research article on turkeys once being worshiped like gods or some other obscure fact, this night I was on a mission. A mission to wade through the bullshit of conspiracy theorists and psychics and self-proclaimed occultists until I found something real.

Until I found an answer.

EIGHT

I must have eventually fallen asleep because I woke up to the sun blasting my eyelids while I lay sprawled on my couch. My bedroom had blackout curtains, so this was not something I was used to or liked at all. An insane, still half-asleep urge to hiss at the sun crept through me.

I rolled off the couch, groaning at the tightness in my back and running my tongue over fuzzy, gross, unbrushed teeth.

There were a whole bunch of missed calls and a text from Val.

Linds? Are you OK? Get back to me ASAP.

My first thought was to ignore her as some petty payback for being kept in the dark by her for so long. Then I remembered she'd been sick and it wasn't her fault.

Then I remembered the raven tattoo.

What the fuck was she thinking getting that? I realized I was coming dangerously close to a double standard—my first tattoo at a rebellious eighteen was Chinese symbols, a bad idea for so many reasons, and one that needed a *lot* of creativity on Rosie's part to suitably cover up—so yeah, it wasn't uncommon to make a poor impulsive decision when it came to tattoos. But the raven, covering her chest? Our *dead* raven?

I couldn't wrap my head around it no matter how hard I tried. Which brought me back around to the research— if you could call it that—I'd done the night before. Had I found anything? Boy, had I. The better question: Was it any good? I had no way of knowing for sure. Really, I'd always been pragmatic. I trusted science and assumed anything unexplained was simply the product of our limitations in knowledge. Eventually, a rational and scientific explanation could be found.

The same would be true of Val. She was happy, more sure of herself than I'd ever seen. Was that really a *problem*? Or was I blindly rejecting her changes because I didn't want things to be different? I could envision a scenario where Val had somewhat of a quarter-life crisis, decided to make a change, take control of her life and be happy. Maybe she dumped Bobby and that was enough weight lifted to be free. And maybe she didn't tell me because she wanted to avoid the *I told you so*. Would I do it? Sadly, I couldn't rule it out.

But the bird. Why the bird? I guessed it could be a symbol, a relatively meaningless way of marking the period in Val's life when she took charge.

I checked the time—just after seven. I needed to be at work by eight, though I had no desire to go, so I texted Donna to say I was sick and staying home. While I waited for a reply I went to the bathroom to clean my tattoo and cover it with antibacterial ointment. The aftercare process was normally something I enjoyed, despite its tedious nature. Taking the time and caring for a new permanent mark on my body, reflecting on the decision and meaning—that was what it was all about. But instead I felt sadness. Not because I regretted getting it, or even because of my mom and the story behind the words inked into my arm. I was sad because Val and her fucking raven tattoo were all my mind could focus on.

When I got back into the living room my phone buzzed and, as expected, it was a pissed-off reply from my boss. No matter. I had the days to use and I was well within company policy to use them. Besides, if I wanted to get technical over it, the unease I'd been feeling the night before had successfully carried over into the morning, making me feel sick to my stomach again. I ignored Donna's vague threats and didn't even bother to respond.

I chugged half a glass of water in one go, thinking about Val again. The more I pondered that alternative explanation of her behavior, the better I felt. Did I buy it completely? No. But it sure as hell made more sense and made me feel better than the batshit crazy scenario fueled by internet wackos I'd formed previously.

There was one way to get to the bottom of it, and that was the source. I texted Val.

Hey, sorry, don't know what came over me. Feeling better though. Lunch at the pub? I took off work just cuz.

Val replied immediately.

Coffee instead? I just quit my job.

NINE

When I got to Mo's Café Val was already there, sitting at a table in the back. Bobby, too. So much for wishful thinking.

"Hey, Val." I took the seat next to her. "Bobby."

I refused to look at him, but I could still feel his eyes on me, knowing he wore a smirk, knowing he relished making me uncomfortable with his presence.

"How're you feeling, Linds?" Val asked.

"I'm fine," I said, waving a hand, dismissing pleasantries. "What the hell is this about you quitting your job?"

Val opened her mouth to speak, but Bobby spoke for her. "She hated that job."

He was always doing that, speaking for her. I ignored him, like I always do.

Val nodded. "It's true."

"Weren't you in line for a promotion soon? Pay raise? Entire office to yourself? An office with a *door* for God's sake?"

"I—"

"She can do better and she knows it. I've been telling her for forever," Bobby said.

I turned to him for the first time. "Will you shut up and let her speak for herself?"

Bobby leaned forward, across the table, his face a scowl, his eyes raging.

"Lindsay, please..." Val said.

I sat back and threw my arms up. "Yeah, fine."

Bobby laughed and shoved back suddenly, his chair squealing on the hardwood floor. He stood, grabbing his wallet from his back pocket. "Whatever. I have to go anyway. Here," he said, tossing a twenty on the table top. "Coffee's on me, ladies."

"Thanks, B," Val said. "I'll see you back home."

He left.

"God, tell me again why you're with that prick?"

"Lindsay—don't."

"I'm serious. He's an asshole."

Val stared into her mug, squeezing it with both hands, absorbing the warmth. "I know he is."

"Then why—"

"Just, don't. Okay? I've got things handled. I promise." Then she smiled at me, that radiant glow I'd seen at Inspired Ink. *New Val.* For the first time, I almost believed her.

We sat quietly for a minute while I looked over the menu and pondered what Val had said. The waitress came over and I ordered a coffee and glazed blueberry muffin. After she brought it I turned to Val, who had been waiting, watching me with soft, observant eyes.

"Did Bobby like your tattoo?"

"Not sure. He doesn't know if he does either. Goes back and forth between feeling weirded out and thinking it's hot." She smirked.

I agreed with part of Bobby's assessment, at least.

"Interesting..."

"Yeah, I think he thinks I'm like a different person with it. Like he's banging around with another chick and it excites him. Which..." She tossed up her shoulders, a gesture I'd have to get used to, apparently.

"Yeah..." I said. "So, tell me then. Why did you quit your job? For real."

Val took a sip of coffee. "Because I had to."

"What does that mean? You *had* to?"

"The job stressed me out. It didn't make me happy."

"What about the promotion?" I tried again. "Pay raise, office, and all that?"

She shook her head. "That promotion was nothing. The pay bump was modest, and the office was located right next to the only bathroom on our floor. My boss knew I was unhappy and tried to appease me. The new title was never going to help my stress levels. If anything, he was going to use that as an excuse to throw more work my way."

"So you quit."

"I did, yeah. I quit my job," she said, laughing. Care-free. *Happy*.

"What are you going to do now? You can't just not work." A thought occurred to me. "Unless Bobby...?"

"Of course not. I'm not relying on Bobby to support me. I'll find something else. Something I like better."

"Just like that?" Skeptical didn't come close to describing my opinion of this line of thinking.

"Sure, why not? Hey, you should quit your job, too! You hate that job, it makes you miserable."

"Val, come on. I can't just quit. I need a paycheck. So do you."

She shrugged. "You'd find something."

As simple as that.

"Well excuse me if I don't share in your optimism," I said, suddenly angry. But what I couldn't tell was whether it was directed at Val for being so easy-going and flippant, or myself for not having the gumption to take initiative and create positive change in my life for once.

"What is up with you? Really," I said.

"I don't know what you're talking about. Nothing is *up with me*," she said, smiling again. I was coming dangerously close to slapping it off her face.

"I'm not kidding. What is going on? First you disappear for days, then—"

"I was sick."

"—you get that fucking raven tattooed on your chest—"

"You said you loved my tat."

"—and now you've quit your job. So maybe you'll forgive me for saying, *what the fuck?*"

My voice had risen above normal volume and I noticed some people staring. I glared back until they looked away. Val's face twitched, the smile faltering momentarily before coming back full shine. She waited a few more seconds, then spoke.

"I don't know what you're talking about."

"Fine." I stood. If she wanted to play it that way, I didn't need to be a part of it. "Tell Bobby thanks for the coffee." I gestured to my nearly full mug. "Better yet, tell him I wasted his money, he'll like that."

I grabbed my jacket and pulled it over my shoulders.

"Where are you going?" Val said.

"I'm leaving, what does it look like?"

"No, stay. Come on, Linds."

"No, you *come on*. If you can't tell me what's going on, or simply won't, then what are we even doing here?"

"Okay, fine. I'll talk to you about it. Just come back. Sit."

I did. I couldn't forget why I asked to meet up in the first place. If she had a story, I needed to listen.

"All right. Go on then," I said.

"It was the bird," Val said. "The dead raven."

The way she said it turned my insides cold. Calling it *ominous* might have been overdramatic, but fuck it, she sounded ominous. On instinct, I took a gulp of coffee, hoping the warm liquid would combat the chill. I didn't know what she was going to say about the bird, but I knew I wouldn't like it. Never mind her annoyingly positive demeanor.

Realizing I hadn't spoken yet and that Val was staring at me, I said, "What about the bird?"

"Something happened when I touched it."

"Wait, you *touched* the bird?"

"I couldn't help it. My fingers…they felt—I don't know? Drawn to it? Sounds crazy, but I think you know. I saw you reaching for it, too."

I thought for a second and realized she was right. I had reached for it. I didn't know why. It grossed me out to think I could have done that.

"Val, what if it was diseased? What if you got rabies or something?"

She laughed, smooth and easy. "Don't be silly. Birds can't get rabies. But…you're not exactly far off either."

"What does that mean?"

"When I touched the raven, it gave me a sort of shock. That's the best way I can describe it. My fingers ached, like I'd been burned."

"Oh yeah, I remember."

"I didn't think too much of it at the time. I'd even sort of convinced myself I hurt them falling to the ground. But I know it was the shock that did it, when I touched the bird. And somehow, for some reason, I think that touch gave me…something."

Val looked down, and I could see embarrassment scribbled across her brow. No surprise she didn't tell me any of this before.

"What something? Come on, you can tell me."

"I'm not sure. Really." She looked up, studying my face, my expression, I assumed discerning whether she should proceed or not. "But, the longer it goes on, the more inclined I am to describe it as a type of *power*."

I scrunched my face. "A power?"

"Yeah, a power. Or gift, maybe? I don't know. I *do* know it sounds crazy, but since then…I just feel like I can do anything. And, more importantly, I want—no, *need*—to be happy. I know I need to rid my life of any negative force."

"Oh, I see," I said, my hackles up in an instant. "You're fucking with me. Unless you honestly expect me to believe this is your superhero origin story."

Val fell back in her chair like I'd slapped her. "That's not what I said. I didn't say I was some kind of super—"

"Yeah, no, I get it. Ha, ha, very funny. Excellent joke. You almost had me there for a minute. *A shock from the bird that gave you a power.* Very clever."

I drained the rest of my coffee and got up to leave again.

"Hey, fuck you, Lindsay."

That stopped me cold. I could have sworn my best friend Val was sitting at the same table with me, but that couldn't have been true. The woman who just spoke, who just said *that*, could not possibly have been one Valerie Thompson.

"Excuse me?"

"You heard me."

"How dare you?"

"No. You got in a tizzy about all this, so I finally tell you what happened and you laugh it off like I'm trying to play a prank. I would've thought I'd earned your trust by now, but apparently not. So, yeah. Fuck you."

This time I did leave, and I left in a rage. Furious with the world, as usual. With Val, who no longer resembled my best friend. And with myself, for being fully aware of the fact that I'd spent the entire night researching curses and hexes and other crazy supernatural shit as an explanation to Val's odd behavior, only to be told by the woman herself that she'd been changed, *affected* somehow by touching the dead raven, and still I refused to believe her.

TEN

Val ignored me again for a few days after that, and this time it was definitely intentional. I couldn't blame her. I spent most of that time working, hating every minute of it and wondering if maybe I had it all wrong.

My brain couldn't make sense of the seemingly inexplicable changes in Val, couldn't reason with the unreality of the supernatural. Hell, the mere existence of God, or a god, or many gods was a coin flip for me on most days; the idea of an afterlife was both appealing and terrifying, and I wouldn't claim to know whether there was one or not.

But for Val, believing without seeing came easy. She wasn't religious, but she was spiritual. Choosing to have faith in something greater, something after. To her, not all mysteries needed an explanation. So, in a way, it kind of made sense. The one bit of rationale I could grasp onto. Val had changed, that was a fact. Why or how she changed was up for debate in my mind, but Val had chosen, once again, to let the supernatural do the heavy lifting. An explanation without actually explaining anything.

Where did that leave us? I wanted a reason. Scratch that—*needed.* I needed the truth. Val's rationale didn't really answer any questions, and while that worked for her, it didn't work for me. But...did that really matter? Regardless of how or why, Val was happy—happier than ever, and I wasn't. I was miserable, really. So who, then, was winning? Was it even possible to have a winner?

I spent the better part of a sleepless night coming to the conclusion that I should let it go, and when I rose out of bed the next morning, exhausted and slightly delirious, I made an extremely hasty decision.

I called my boss, told her I quit, and hung up before she had a chance to respond.

And it felt amazing.

A flood of power and anxious energy washed over me.

I skipped around my apartment, singing and dancing and running to the fridge to grab a beer because why the hell not?

Then, as if the crack of the can's seal manifested the release valve of my good vibes, I became instantly deflated. The reality of my decision knocked the wind out of me. Suddenly, the entirety of my internal debates and their conclusion last night went out the window.

What had I done? I had nothing lined up. What the hell was I going to do? I needed money. I needed to pay rent, buy food, *live*.

I felt panicked, and it hurt. I remembered Val with her happy-go-lucky aura and tried to force that calm positivity back into my own body. It had been there just a moment ago. Could I snatch it from the air and suck it back in?

I had to call Val. I needed to tell her what I did and have her tell me what I had to do to stay as happy as she was. In my whirlwind of emotions, I considered a possible return to Rosy Mound Natural Area. Was the ritual site still there? I could touch the raven and be transformed like her, willfully ignoring the insanity of doing so.

When I grabbed my phone it was already ringing.

Val.

"Hey, I was just about—"

"Where are you?"

"—to call you. I just quit my job and at first it felt wonderful and I was so—"

"Lindsay—"

"—excited, but then suddenly it vanished. Poof. Gone. I don't—"

"Lindsay!" she yelled, stopping my words short. Then, whispering, she said, "Shut up, for just a second. Okay? I need your help."

"Yeah, sure. Sorry," I said. "Help with what?"

"Bobby's dead. I—"

"Bobby's what?"

"—killed him. And I need your help with the body."

ELEVEN

I drove in spurts of adrenaline-fueled *holy shit fuck what is going on* over the speed limits and absolute terror-stricken *ohmygod oh my god what if a cop pulls me over what do I say* under the speed limits, all the while repeating the rest of the phone conversation with Val in my head.

It wasn't hard. She hadn't said much.

"Val," I'd said, slowly, "what are you talking about?"

"Come to Hidden Lake Preserve. Right now. We have work to do."

Then she'd hung up.

I replayed what she said not because I thought I'd missed something in her words, but because of the way she said them.

Calm. Unemotional. Urgent without pleading.

We have work to do.

Hidden Lake was across town from my apartment, which normally would have been a bitch for traffic. But it was still only seven in the morning when I hit the road, on a Saturday no less. Traffic was nonexistent.

I arrived thirty minutes on the dot after Val hung up. The parking lot at Hidden Lake was empty save for two cars—one I didn't recognize, and a red Jeep I knew to be Bobby's. I parked next to the Jeep and got out, looking for Val. I looked for Bobby, too, still pretty sure he had to be alive, and that I might be walking into some kind of fucked up payback. She wasn't there and hadn't told me on the phone exactly where she'd be, but I knew. There was only one place at Hidden Lake Preserve she would be.

Our spot.

It was a place Val and I found off the beaten path a couple years before, while trying to avoid people. No surprise, the popular spot to go at Hidden Lake Preserve was down the main trail off the parking lot through the woods to Hidden Lake. So, we went the opposite way, taking the trail across the prairie that made a big loop out over some rolling hills and back to the parking lot. Except, about a third of the way down the prairie trail it came up on another stand of trees toward the western edge of the preserve, and after a short detour off the path, there was a game trail that led down into a shallow ravine, along a trickling creek, and back up the slope to a small clearing.

I didn't know what happened with Val and Bobby, but any scenario I could possibly imagine could only have happened at or near our spot.

I made my way across the prairie, half walking, half running. It felt weird, making that trek to what I assumed would be the most bizarre, fucked up situation in my life.

For some reason I expected the weather to be wild, a storm brewing or raging or—whatever, like in the movies. But no, the weather that morning was downright tranquil. Lazy wisps of clouds that did nothing to block the rising sun. A lack of wind so total, the shin-high prairie grass wasn't even wavering.

That morning was dead calm and peaceful.

A lot like Val had been.

When I crested the ravine bank and reached the clearing, Val was sitting on the trunk of a downed tree at the back, staring up into the sky, one leg crossed gently over the other. The moment I saw her I erupted with all the questions pent up in my head.

"Val, are you okay? What happened? Was it an accident?"

She dropped her gaze to me, watching me enter the clearing, but didn't respond right away. I took the moment to fully take in the scene before me.

My eyes and brain registered Bobby first, face down on the ground. Next, I saw the hole off to my left—a mound of dirt piled along its edge—but didn't immediately understand what it meant. My mind was fuzzy and buzzing. Then I saw the shovel at Val's feet, and with it came a heart-sinking revelation.

This was no accident. Val killed Bobby, and she had planned it. Had she planned my involvement, too?

She stood.

Before she could speak, I blurted out, "What did you do? What the *fuck*, did you do?"

"I killed him. What does it look like?"

"But—But why?"

Val huffed, as if my confusion and horror were an annoyance to her. "I'm surprised at you, Linds. You, of all people, should understand. Bobby was a worthless human being. An asshole. Scum," she said, then actually spit on the ground, disgusted.

"Well, yeah. He was all those things, sure. But," I shook my head, "did he deserve to die?"

I was asking that question as much for myself as I was for Val. *Did* Bobby deserve to die? He absolutely was the embodiment of human trash. He was mean, sadistic, an abuser, and I firmly believed he didn't deserve to walk on this earth, let alone date Val. But. Just because he didn't deserve to live a life where he could constantly torment everyone around him...did that mean he deserved to be wiped from the planet completely? And was it Val's right to make that choice? To *kill* another human being, even if it *was* Bobby?

I had to admit to myself, this shit was much murkier and grayer than it sounded in my college ethics class.

"You were always telling me to get rid of him, saying you never understood why I could be with a guy like Bobby. Saying that I deserved better. Well, I don't think I ever truly disagreed with you, but I know now just how right you were."

"Hold on. Are you trying to put this on me? Are you saying you did this because of things I said? That is some bullshit, Val, and you know it."

She shrugged, her focus shifting away, enraging me more. "Semantics. But we can discuss it later if you'd like. Right now we have work to do. We need to take care of this mess."

"Whoa, wait a minute. Who says I'm helping? Sorry, but this one is all you. I can't get involved in…in *murder*, for fuck's sake."

Val was standing next to Bobby's corpse now, one hand on her hip, the other pointing at Bobby. "You're really going to be okay with him taking me down? You're going to let him win?"

"Val, he can't win…He's dead."

"You know what I mean. Are you helping me or not?"

"Fuuuck. This *new you* or whatever is a real son of a bitch, you know that?"

Val didn't respond, only stared indifferently.

"Ugh. God. Fine. I'll help you with *this*, and only this. Nothing more, ever again. And…after it's over…I don't know if we can be—"

"Shut up and get over here."

I edged closer to her and the body, half wanting and half dreading the possibility of Bobby suddenly lurching up, leaping at me. *Surprise!*

But no, Bobby wasn't moving. I was no expert, but a large pool of blood leeching into the ground beneath a prone, motionless body didn't inspire hope that said body was still alive.

"What did you…uhh—what happened?"

"Do you really want to know?" she asked.

"I don't know," I responded. "Probably not, but I guess I should, since I'm fucking balls deep in it now."

"I sliced his neck open," she said, shrugging. She held up a pocket knife, then gestured to the ground around the body. "He bled out in a matter of minutes. Easy."

"Jesus Christ," I whispered.

"What side do you want?" Val asked, oblivious to my shock and horror.

"I'm sorry, what?" My mind was frantic, searching for something, anything, to make this make sense—but it came up blank.

"What *side*. Arms or legs? We need to carry him to the hole. Or do you wanna flip for it?"

"Oh God…His legs, I guess."

"All right. Let's get to it, then. Come on."

I approached the body, skirting the circle of blood as best I could, then reached down for Bobby's ankles. Val was around by his head, hooking her hands under his armpits.

"Count of three," she said. "One, two…three."

We hefted the body. Of course I knew the phrase *dead weight*, but still, I was not prepared for how heavy it would be. We both struggled, our feet scuffling across the ground, but we made it to the hole.

For some reason I wanted to lay Bobby down gently, but as soon as we were over the hole, Val simply let go, in effect forcing me to drop him, too. He landed with a great whump. I stepped back immediately, my hands feeling dirty, *tainted*, longing for the bottle of hand sanitizer sitting in my glove compartment.

Val retrieved the shovel and methodically dug up the ground where Bobby's blood had pooled and soaked in. With each shovelful, she walked a couple steps and tossed it on the body.

"What about the knife?" I asked. "Aren't you going to bury it, too?"

Val laughed. "It'd be pretty silly to bury the murder weapon with the victim. Believe it or not, I'm trying *not* to get caught."

"Oh. Right… So what are you going to do with it?"

She stopped mid-shovel and said, "What, do you want it for evidence against me?"

"What? No, that's not what I meant. I just—"

She broke my rambling with a barking, throaty laugh. "I'm messing with you, Linds." Then she locked eyes with me. "You wouldn't do that. You're not going to turn me in."

When she looked away and resumed burying Bobby, I gasped to catch my breath. I didn't know when I started holding it, but I hadn't been breathing. And suddenly my skin felt warm, tingly. Embarrassment? I couldn't tell. Had Val just threatened me? It seemed like it, although I couldn't be sure.

I was sweating heavily, even though we were still in shade and the air was cool. Val, too, her tattooed raven's eye glistening, playing tricks on me again.

While she continued filling up the shallow hole where Bobby had died and bled out, I tore my gaze away to glance worriedly around for onlookers. She was nearly finished. Thank God, we were almost done. I looked around the clearing, searching for anything out of place, then looked back to Val patting the dirt down to an even grade with the forest floor.

Watching her move quickly, but efficiently, tidying up, triggered a memory of the time I found her cleaning up the shards of a plate Bobby had thrown at her at a party. How surreal, seeing it again at the scene of a crime—the scene of a *murder*—except with more calm and determination. Then suddenly, I was certain, as if the thought had only just occurred to me. No matter what I thought before, if there had been any doubt, it was gone now. I would not turn Val in. I wouldn't jeopardize her freedom for the sake of Bobby. Even more, I resolved to help her in whatever way possible. It felt good to be certain about something.

Val smoothed out the dirt, then expertly messed it up again to avoid it looking *too* neat. She spread several handfuls of last year's dead leaves and other plant litter across the disrupted patch of ground, then for good measure swung a few dead branches askew across Bobby's ad hoc burial plot.

She stepped away from the site carefully, gathering her shovel and bag, dusting off her hands on her pants.

"Now what do we do?" I asked, needing to know but afraid to hear the answer just the same.

"I'm going to take Bobby's Jeep and you're going to follow me up north so that we can stage his disappearance."

TWELVE

By the time I got back to my apartment, it was late enough for dinner, but I turned down Val's offer to grab a bite. I had zero appetite, and zero desire to spend any more time with her. All I wanted to do was open a bottle of whiskey and drink myself stupid.

She didn't tell me where exactly we were going, just *north*, so I ended up following her more than an hour up into the heart of the Manistee National Forest, winding down rural highways, then onto bare, little used back roads until eventually stopping at a trailhead. She parked on the road, then got out and told me to stay where I was while she drove Bobby's Jeep into the parking area and walked back. She said she didn't want multiple sets of tire tread tracks.

I hate to admit it, but she knew what she was doing. It was creepy how well she was handling everything.

On the drive back, Val told me in much greater detail what had happened out at Hidden Lake Preserve, apparently unconcerned about what I might do or who I might tell now that I had all the info on her crime. She told me about how she had come to the realization that Bobby was a monster, and not only did he not deserve to be with her, but that he didn't deserve to be with any other woman ever. Or even *to be* at all.

Then Val went into excruciating detail about her final night with Bobby, how she let him *have her*—her words—one last time despite her disgust for the man, toying with him because she knew the power dynamic had shifted, knew what was to come for the bastard. Then she convinced Bobby to take a sunrise hike at Hidden Lake with her, referencing some innate ability to manipulate I had no idea about, and directed him out to our spot—where she'd even planned far enough ahead to stash a shovel.

When they reached the clearing—Bobby a step ahead of her—she quickly pulled out her pocket knife, flicked it open, and slit his throat.

"It was easier than I expected," she said, "letting the sharp blade and its metal teeth do the brunt of the work. Like slicing into a medium-rare steak."

All the while I wondered who was really sitting beside me, delving into extremely sensitive information, and knowing for certain that it was not my friend Val. That chick was long gone. What I was less certain about, however, was whether this new person fascinated me or terrified me. Perhaps both.

Val did nearly all the talking on the drive back, clearly happy to gab, but at one point I asked, "Are you really...changed?" because truthfully, I still didn't know what was going on with her.

"Of course I am. The raven gave me the power to be happy." Then she smiled.

"Were you happy when you were killing Bobby?" I blurted.

"Yes, of course I was."

Part of me expected that answer, but I still didn't know what to say to that, so I remained silent the rest of the way. I didn't even respond when we got to her apartment and she said, while getting out of my car, "See you later, Linds."

At home I sat, drinking straight from my fifth of Jack, thinking but wanting not to think about what I'd seen. I thought about Val's insistence that she could get what she wanted, that she had an ability to be convincing beyond normal human capacity, and how absurd that sounded. Yet, as much as I didn't want to admit it, I had evidence. I saw it happen with my own eyes. We were still covered in dirt and grime when we got back to the parking lot and ran into a hiker. He'd said hi, and Val responding with, "You didn't see us. You're the only person here." How fucking insane of a thing was that to say out loud to another human being with true sincerity? But the elderly man laughed and nodded and continued to his car, mumbling something that sure fucking sounded like, "Surprised no one else is here this morning."

Not to mention there was no way Bobby would have willingly gone out to Hidden Lake so early in the morning.

Then—oh then—there was that thing she said to me. *You're not going to turn me in.*

Hadn't I decided that on my own? Or had she used a bizarre new power to persuade me? To prevent me from going to the police and tattling on her? Despite everything I'd seen so far, I still couldn't let my mind go there. Not yet.

Before I knew it, night had come, and I was left drinking in the darkness of my apartment. Half the fifth of whiskey was gone, which I knew would be bad when I tried to stand. For the moment, though, I felt fine. Good even, as long as I kept my mind blank. Briefly contented, I wanted nothing more than to freeze in time and simply exist. Drunk and surrounded by darkness.

I made the mistake of looking at my phone and catching the time. I groaned. Nearly midnight. And I had to get up early the next morning because I made the dumbass mistake of picking up the Sunday shift at work...

Then I remembered I'd quit my job. That very morning. An eon ago.

"Oh my God. Holy shit, what did I do?" I said to no one. I stood, then my woozy legs dropped me back on the couch. I stood again, but didn't know what I was doing or where I was going. I grabbed my head with both hands and groaned again, drawing it out until it became a growl. The thought that I could have felt any amount of happiness from dropping my only source of income seemed impossible now.

Maybe because I was severely intoxicated, I laughed. A thought struck me: even if I hadn't quit my job, there was no chance I could handle a day of work. Not with the way things had been going there, and especially not with what I'd seen earlier.

I thought of that thing my mother always told me, and for once in my life, it connected. *Never worry about something you can't fix in the moment.* I always chalked it up to some silly platitude, a thing mothers said. But now, I wondered if I'd been wrong all this time. Why worry about my job or Val or Bobby or curses or whatever supernatural bullshit was maybe going on, right at this moment? I couldn't change any of them in the middle of the night. I couldn't get my job back or start another one. I couldn't bring Bobby back from the dead, even if I wanted to, which I didn't. I couldn't magically change Val back to the person I knew and loved.

What I could do, however, was keep slugging away at the whiskey until I passed out. No more thoughts, no more worries.

Of course, that wasn't how it worked. Not for me, anyway. The more I drank, the more I thought about it, the more I worried about *everything*.

About the time my bottle was nearing empty and my brain was nearing the blackness, I gave some true drunken consideration to what I should do next.

The drunk part of me wanted to pack a bag and hit the road. Leave it all behind.

But the *really* drunk part of me was closer to the truth of the matter, which was that I missed my best friend. That part of me, deep down, believed something happened to Val, and fuck if I wasn't going to find out what. I couldn't let her simply slip away from me. I still spent most days thinking about how I failed to be there for my mom, failed to see the warning signs. Well, these were Val's warning signs.

Right then I knew I was going to do whatever it took to get my best friend back or die trying.

THIRTEEN

The booze rooster had me up at an obscene hour the next morning. I only remembered about half of the night prior, but it was enough. I remembered I made a plan of sorts, to stick with Val and figure out as much as I could about this new version of her. I still couldn't fully buy into the curse, not yet, but I knew no matter the cause, Val believed she had changed.

I chugged a Gatorade and forced myself to eat some toast before brushing away the scum from the past twenty-four hours. I probably should have showered, still reeking of whiskey, but I didn't feel like it. I added an extra layer of deodorant instead.

I walked out the door as the sun rose above the trees and hopped in my car. The radio DJ was rambling off local news, so I reached to change the station, but froze at the words coming through my speakers.

"—authorities say they found the body of an uniden- tified male. They haven't released much in the way of details yet, but an alley along the four hundred block of Division where the body was found has been cordoned off."

I smashed the volume button to silence the radio, exhaling a gasp of relief so intense my chest shook. Thank Christ. Opposite side of town as the preserve. Definitely not Bobby.

Driving on to Val's apartment, I thought multiple times about shooting her a warning text to let her know I was heading her way, but figured she owed me one with her morning call to clean up a murder the day before. And besides, I thought I might learn something about this new Val if I could catch her off guard.

I should have known I couldn't surprise Val. She answered two seconds after I buzzed.

"Lindsay?"

"Yeah…how did you know?"

"Who else would it be? Bobby?" Her laugh was cutoff as she released the intercom button and unlocked the front door.

I hurried upstairs and entered her place to find her sipping a mug of coffee at the kitchen table. On cue, Patch came running. I gave him a cursory pet as I closed the door. "I wouldn't be making jokes about Bobby like that."

The news about the body found was still fresh on my mind and I shuddered involuntarily.

She laughed again, then shrugged. So goddamned calm. She couldn't be bothered to care, as if she held sway over how humanity and the universe behaved.

"What *are* you going to do about Bobby, though?" I asked.

"I don't need to do anything. I already did it. He's dead."

"Val, you know what I mean."

"All right, yeah. Relax, okay? Sheesh. I'm going to wait until tonight and call the police. File a missing persons report, or whatever."

"Do you think that'll work?"

"Why wouldn't it? I'll tell the police he stayed with me Friday night, which is true, then left my apartment really early Saturday morning—which is also technically true. They don't need to know I left with him. I'll say that he's been flaky before—also true—but that he hasn't responded to any of my texts or calls—I keep trying, for evidence—in almost two days. Eventually they'll find his car, but at that point, who cares? I'm sure eventually I'll have to lie to the police again, but really, I'm not worried about that." Nonchalant, calm, collected. Rinse, lather, repeat. Then, deciding that portion of the conversation was over, she said, "There's still coffee in the pot, if you want some. You know where the mugs are."

I didn't know what to say. Truthfully, it sounded like she had it under control. And I did want coffee, so I got some, then returned to sit with her at the table.

"I thought you said you didn't want to see me after yesterday, or some nonsense like that," she said.

"Yeah, well. I guess that wasn't true." I sipped the scalding coffee, feeling uncomfortable and off my game already. "I'm here now—"

"Because you want to know how I changed."

"Yeah…how'd you know?"

"How could I not? I've never been happier and you're miserable. Of course you'd want to know about my transfiguration."

"Well I wouldn't exactly put it that way," I said, then added, "Did you say *transfiguration?*"

Val ignored my question. "Well, I already told you. You just weren't listening."

If she was mad I couldn't tell, but she'd done a good job of setting me off down my own path of anger. I forced myself to take another drink of coffee and remember why I was there.

"You're right. I wasn't listening. I guess I just…didn't want to listen. It's hard to accept this sort of thing, you know?"

"For some," she said absently.

I closed my eyes and took a breath before I said what I was thinking.

"Fine. How about you tell me again? I'd like to know all about your…*transfiguration*. Don't leave anything out. I really do want to know."

She looked at me, across the table. "You do?"

I nodded, staring back.

"Okay then. Where do I start? The beginning again?"

"Sure, why not? Did you leave anything out the first time? Maybe stretch the truth?"

She shook her head once, then stopped. "Well…now that you mention it, I probably wasn't entirely truthful. But!" she said, holding up a hand, "Before you think I lied, that's not what I mean."

"You're talking in circles. What do you mean?"

"See, that's just it. I'm not entirely sure. Maybe that as time goes on, I'm learning more about what has already and is yet to change in me? I told you before that when I touched the raven, I felt a shock, like *something* was transferring into me. I know I said it was a *gift* or *power* before, but I'm not sure I even fully believed what I was saying. Now, though, I know that's *exactly* what it was."

She'd been looking down at her hands while she spoke but lifted her eyes to meet mine now. They were glowing— not literally, but they might as well have been. Initially I was startled, but as the moment passed, the feeling was replaced by fascination. I couldn't help but be drawn in. Val exuded intensity, but the kind you absorbed to become energized.

She continued: "The raven gave me a power. Or powers, I guess. All of which are rooted in happiness and the desire, above all else, to be happy. This new power has taught me how, given me the ability to rid my life of anything negatively affecting my happiness. It's given me *control.*"

"Control?" I asked, hearing the echoes of previous, worrying thoughts. "Over yourself?"

Val bobbed her head side to side, as if weighing my choice of words. "Sure, but also over everything."

I laughed, but she wasn't joking. Of course she wasn't. How could I think so? Because it was absurd, I guess.

Not absurd—insane.

"Come on. *Everything?* That's a bit overdramatic, don't you think?"

"You don't have to believe me. But you asked for the truth, and I'm giving it to you."

"Look, you won't sell me on *everything,* but fine, let's say you have more control over…things. Care to share some proof of that?"

She pondered my question for a minute, then said, "Sure, I can tell you about something you'll understand."

I ignored her patronizing words and tone. "Go on."

"Okay, so you know how I quit my job and you were concerned, to say the least?" I nodded. "And I told you I wasn't worried, I'd find something else. Well, I did. I have a new job."

"Wait, really? How?"

"Yep. I cold called that legal firm down the block from my old job. You know the one I said I wanted to get into a while back? I asked for an interview right there. They agreed and ended up hiring me on the spot. They said they loved my energy and confidence."

She shrugged—always fucking shrugging—and smiled, as if to say, *it's no big thing.*

"Bullshit."

"No joke. I start tomorrow."

I shook my head in disbelief, but not without fascination. Frankly, I was impressed.

"What else?" I asked.

"People keep giving me free stuff."

"Like what?"

"Coffee at Mo's. Drinks from The Grand, and not from skeevy dudes either—the bartenders give me free drinks."

"For free," I said. "No questions asked?"

"Yeah, just like that," she responded, but she wasn't looking at me anymore.

I sat back in my chair and let the silence ride out for a couple minutes. Clearly, something was off there. At first, I attributed it to my general skepticism, but it was more than that. Like Val was still only telling me part of the story. She'd gone out of her way to say she hadn't told the entire truth before, but I no longer believed she said that for transparency's sake. She was trying to further her deception.

I didn't tell you everything before, but now I am, see? Honesty.

I wasn't buying it. But what, exactly, wasn't she telling me? Impossible to know, but I tried for the truth again, this time with a different line of questioning to see if I could tease out more details.

I said, "Do you think I could change or transform or whatever, too?"

"I don't think so."

"Why not?"

She shrugged.

"What if I went back to the dunes, touched the raven like you did?"

"I doubt it's still there. And who's to say it would work the same?"

"Why not?" I repeated.

She shrugged again. "I have a feeling it wouldn't, is all."

"A feeling...right. *Why,* Val?"

She shook her head. "Nothing."

"No, something. Come on. Out with it."

"Well, I don't know. I just don't think you'd be very receptive."

"What's that supposed to mean?" I asked, immediately defensive.

"Linds, you know exactly what I mean. You don't *believe* in anything. Like, seriously nothing. Whereas I've always been open to the unexplained."

"I am open," I protested, but her *are you serious* stare said what I was thinking. She was right, of course. But was she saying it because she meant it? Or because she wanted to convince me I couldn't have what she had? Like the *gift* was hers, and hers alone.

"I mean, really. Lindsay, dear. You're still trying to deny everything I've told you about myself. You're as closed minded to anything out of the ordinary as it gets. For all we know you were *supposed* to change, just like me, but you shut it out. Maybe the raven knew you didn't deserve it."

"Excuse me? And *you* did? You deserved to find happiness while I get to stay miserable? Is that what you think?"

"That's not what I said—"

"No, it is. That's exactly what you said. And here's the kicker, if all I'm going to ever be is miserable, won't that have a *negative effect on your happiness* or whatever? What are you going to do, kill me too?"

I was standing—though I didn't know when I stood—my hands gripping the back of the chair so tightly my skin stretched white over my knuckles, my face flushed with red heat. Always so tense in Val's presence now. I said those things because I was mad, but also, a part of me wondered if in Val's eyes I shared a similar position to Bobby. Not that I thought so lowly of myself that I'd consider myself equal to him, but still. I didn't know what Val thought anymore. Hell, maybe I *was* her next victim, the next bit of negative dead weight needing to be excised.

Val stood now, too. Calm and deliberate. When she spoke, it was softly, but with maddeningly assured confidence. "Lindsay, look at me. You do *not* deserve to be miserable. Okay? You wanted to know what I thought, and I told you. I simply believe my personality is more in line and receptive to the strange. If you think I'm wrong, that's fine, we can disagree. But, there's nothing we can do to prove it now. The ritual site is gone. Long gone.

"We're still us, though. Okay? You're you and I'm still me. Just…a newer, happier version. That's all. And for heaven's sake, I would never kill you. Unless you did something silly and tried to ruin my happiness." She said it with a wink, then walked down the hall to the bathroom without another word.

When she came back, she didn't say *just kidding* or anything, not that I expected her to. But it was the final confirmation I needed—no matter what Val said, I was a friend until I wasn't. Until I became a threat.

In Val's eyes, I was expendable.

FOURTEEN

The following Wednesday evening, I got a call from Val. I hadn't heard from her much since that last visit—I assumed it was because she was busy with her new job—but I didn't exactly mind either. I didn't want Val to know something was up, because I still had grand plans of *fixing* her, whatever that entailed. But, things were clearly different between us whether she realized it or not.

Besides, I was busy cleaning up my own damn mess. Miraculously, I managed to quit my job during the lull period in the month, but in a couple weeks several bills were due. I needed to find work. Or a briefcase full of money. On the one hand, I had no degree and no highly trained skills of any kind; on the other my last job had been managing staff at a retail clothing store—I wasn't an architect, but I couldn't go back to the grease pit of a fast-food joint. Yet. I knew I was being picky, and that only added to the stress.

So, I was hesitant when I saw Val's face light up my phone, but I answered anyway.

"Hey, what's up?"

"I just got done talking to the police. They're going to want to talk to you, so expect them soon."

"Wait, what? What the fuck, Val. Really?"

"Oh, calm down, will you? My God you're so dramatic. I told them I hung out with you Saturday morning at Hidden Lake Preserve after Bobby left my apartment. Which, as you remember, is *true*. I told them we met at the preserve around 7:30, walked for a bit, then went for a cruise around town since the weather was nice. That's it. Just repeat those simple facts. Got it? Everything will be fine, I promise. Okay?"

"Yeah, sure… *Okay*, I mean." And I did mean it. I was still freaking out pretty good inside, but it was reassuring to have Val be so calm and confident. I didn't like the thought of having to lie to the police, but if I stuck to the simple facts, as Val said, I would technically be telling the truth. Lying by omission, sure, but that was semantics.

"Great. I'm guessing they'll call, but they asked for your address, too, so I gave them that. Maybe they'll stop by."

"Gee, thanks Val."

"Like they wouldn't have figured it out anyway."

"I guess you're right," I said. "Was that all?" I know it sounded kind of rude, but I was still in the mode of wanting to keep our interactions brief.

"Actually, no," Val said. "Do you think you can do me a favor?"

"Sure?" Not actually sure if I could or even wanted to.

"I'm headed out of town for the rest of the week for a work trip. I leave first thing tomorrow morning and won't be back until Sunday afternoon. Can you check in on Patch for me while I'm gone?"

"Oh. Yeah, of course," I said, relieved at the simple request.

"Thanks. He'll probably be happier to have you there than me. That dumb cat loves you. Maybe you should just keep him."

I laughed, but Val didn't. "You're not serious...?"

Now she laughed, "Of course not. He's my furball, and he sees you all the time, anyway."

"Right," I said, suddenly uncomfortable. "So, how'd you manage a work trip already? You just started."

"Another lady from the office was supposed to go, but she had an unfortunate incident pop up. Lucky for me," Val said, and I could hear her grinning. "My employer already paid for everything anyway, so now I get to go."

My insides contracted and my mouth suddenly went dry. She wouldn't have done anything to her coworker, would she? I wasn't sure I could rule it out.

I swallowed hard. "Yeah, lucky you."

"Guess where they're sending me."

"I don't know, up north somewhere?"

"San Diego."

"No way."

"Going to Cali, baby!" she screamed into the phone, then laughed.

"Damn," I said, but nothing more, unsure if I'd be able to hide my jealousy.

"Should I drop my spare key off at your place? I'm at home right now, but I'm heading downtown later for a drink with a coworker. He's cute, by the way," she whispered, then laughed again.

"Wow, getting right after it, huh?" I hated the thinly veiled resentment in my voice. "But you can drop the key off here if that works. I'll be home all night, just searching for jobs…"

"Oh girl, you'll find something soon. I just know it."

"I hope so. I'll see you later, then."

I hung up, wondering where I went so wrong. I should have felt happy about everything going right in Val's life. Instead, I felt anger and even a little bit of hatred. Despite knowing my feelings were fucked up, I couldn't help it. I felt like the polar opposite of Val, like her happiness was sucking all of my happiness out of me. Like she was feeding off it.

I laughed humorlessly, shaking my head at the image. A joy-sucking vampire. A murderous one, to boot.

FIFTEEN

Thursday evening rolled around, and the cops had yet to call. The anticipation was dreadful, to the point of wanting to get the damn thing over with already. I decided to head to Val's for a distraction. She said I didn't need to stop by until Friday—she'd given Patch a pile of food before she left, and he was a grazer, not a gorger—but really I had nothing better to do, anyway. I'd seemingly exhausted the list of potential jobs to apply for. And since Patch seemed like the only friend I had at the moment, I craved his attention. Perhaps that was pathetic, but I didn't much care.

Val was gone. That was the important part. I knew I'd feel infinitely more comfortable in her apartment than I had when she was around.

And I'd have a chance to snoop.

When I got inside, thinking about what exactly I might find that could help me help Val, Patch rushed me, rubbing up against my legs with an arched back and quivering tail.

"Hey, Punky Patch," I said, scratching his back. "Auntie Linds is here to hang out. I don't suppose your mom left me anything to drink in the fridge, huh?"

Patch meowed, as if he understood perfectly what I'd asked him. I set my backpack down and went to the fridge. On the handle was a note:

L – Beer in the fridge, popcorn on the counter. Crash in the guest room if you drink too much. Stay safe. Thx! – V

A pang of sorrow rang inside my ribcage but was followed quickly with a chime of hope. This note was one hundred percent Val. *My* Val, not that new and not-so-improved joy-hungry Val of the past couple weeks. I pulled the sticky note from the fridge and stuck it in my back pocket, wanting to hold on to the piece of the best friend I loved, who I missed, wanting a reminder of what I would be fighting for.

The sorrow was almost enough to guilt me into abandoning my plans to search the place—but only *almost*. I spent a good half hour opening drawers and cabinets, digging through Val's closet and under her bed, but ultimately I had no clue what I was looking for, and nothing remotely relevant stood out.

Annoyed and not a little bored, I went and grabbed a beer from the six-pack—she'd left my favorite, of course—popped the top, and proceeded to drink about half in one swig. I hadn't planned on crashing at Val's, but I had my computer in my bag, where I also always carried a toothbrush, so the idea was starting to sound nice. Knock back a few more beers—okay, all the beers—pop a bag of corn, and watch a movie on Netflix while getting snuggles from my main dude. Even if said dude was a fat, fuzzball cat.

My phone rang as I settled into the couch. For a second, I hoped it was Val. I had the urge to talk to her, like in the old days. Just chat about anything, or nothing. But it was an unknown number, so I dismissed it.

Patch made his way to my lap. I sat, stroking him absently, thinking about how maybe *I* should call *her*. But I told myself she was busy. While probably true, it wasn't my real reason. I knew if I called and she had time to chat, it wouldn't be the same. It wouldn't be the Val I wanted.

Scanning through Netflix, title to title, I did my usual song and dance trying to figure out what to watch. There were probably forty shows and movies on my to-watch list, that I somehow was never in the mood for. I was still searching when I went for a second beer, and that decided things. Chances were low that I'd still be paying close attention in an hour, so something new was off the table. So, like so many times before, I settled on a movie I'd seen a hundred times.

The Princess Diaries.

I'd seen it for the first time as a kid during the fucked-up period in my life when my dad left. It let me dream of a better life. A chance to escape the shitty one I was stuck in. It gave me the optimism I needed then, and it'll always be a comfort movie. No matter what kind of edgy, *take no shit* persona I try to carry, *The Princess Diaries* will always make me feel warm, even hopeful that the world isn't all bad.

I wanted to get wrapped up in the movie. Just pet the cat and recite every line as if they were the very words my brain had always known and wanted to say.

But, as I should have known, that didn't exactly happen. A little more than an hour and a couple beers later, things started to fall apart on me. When the movie's main character, Mia, started to get popular and invited to all those events, and subsequently neglected her best friend... yeah. I cried.

Every other time I'd seen the film, I'd connected most with Mia. I wanted to be her. This time was different. This time I felt like her abandoned best friend, Lilly. A rather childish metaphor for my life at the moment, but hey, blame it on the alcohol.

Which I did. I finished the last swallow of my open beer, then vowed to leave the remaining two in the fridge. I shut off the movie, too, and got up to walk around the apartment, stretch my legs, and work out of my wallowing.

What I really wanted was some weed. I was an occasional smoker, but when I did, it did wonders to calm me down and make me more cheerful. At the very least, complacent.

Problem was, how to get it? I didn't have any on me and I was definitely too drunk to drive anywhere—

"Oh shit," I said out loud, too loud, spooking Patch off the couch and causing him to scurry over to his cat tree. "Oops, sorry buddy!" I called to him, then closed my eyes, concentrating on what had interrupted my train of thought, what would hopefully solve my current problem. I had completely forgotten, until that moment, that Val *had* smoked weed. And, if I was lucky, she'd have some lying around.

I thought back to the conversation several months earlier with Val over a nightcap in Tony's Pub. I didn't remember what prompted it exactly, probably a random snide comment about Bobby, but for whatever reason, instead of defending him, Val leaned over her beer and whispered to me. "I have a stash of weed in my apartment I smoke sometimes after Bobby leaves."

Though legal to partake in Michigan, it was still a shocking admission coming from her. I'd said, "No way. Val! Wait—does he know?"

"Oh, God no. He'd freak out on me if he ever found out. So, you can't tell him!"

"You know I wouldn't tell that motherfucker anything. Where'd you stash it?"

"Behind that air return vent thing in the living room."

In her living room now, I spun in a slow circle until I spotted the vent. I went to it, wondering where she kept her screwdriver, then noticed the vent was already hanging a bit loose. I tugged at it once, and the whole thing came away, the screws having been stripped out and barely holding it in place. Some hiding place.

The hole in the wall was low to the floor and the room was dark, so from my kneeling position I couldn't immediately see anything. I laid flat to get a better look, only to find a bend in the duct. Reluctantly, feeling like I was about to stick my hand into a spider nest, I reached inside and around the corner.

I patted around fruitlessly for a few seconds before brushing something solid. Definitely not a baggy of weed. Still, I was intrigued. I grasped the object and pulled it from inside the duct.

A stone, about the size of my palm. At first glance, I could tell it was flat, gray, and smooth, but otherwise featureless. A kick ass skipping stone, no doubt, but I couldn't fathom why Val would have hidden it in there. If anything, I assumed it was hidden back before Val ever moved to this apartment, probably by a kid who didn't want their older brother to steal it.

I continued to stroke the stone, liking the way my fingers glided across its smooth surface, like it was a giant version of the worry stones I used to get from touristy knick-knack shops growing up. Practically entranced, I made my way to the kitchen where there was more light, still rubbing the rock down. I was so rapt, I started to feel almost dirty doing it, but I was alone, so who cared?

I flipped the stone over and in fact, *not* featureless. The indentations scraped against the pads of my fingers, but I might as well have been trying to read braille. I settled directly below the light over the kitchen sink and held the stone up to my face.

What I saw made me gasp and drop it like the thing had been buried in a bed of coals and was much too hot to hold. It clunked and clanged around in the stainless-steel sink, sending Patch running around the apartment again.

The stone had an engraving, all right. A drawing.

A raven in flight.

SIXTEEN

I picked the stone up from the sink. Delicately—holding it between my thumb and pointer finger like I would a hornet by the wing, unsure if it was truly dead, afraid it would use the rest of its life to sting me.

Another damn raven. Etched in stone and hidden away like contraband.

The question now was, where had it come from? A modicum of thought provided the only likely answer. The ritual site, of course.

I remembered, then, how Val had bent to the bundle one last time as I walked away. She'd claimed it was to cover the bird back up, which she may well have, but I had a suspicion that she'd seen the stone and wanted to take it without me knowing. Why she kept it from me, though, I wasn't sure.

As I examined the stone further, I noticed an engraved two-word caption below the raven.

FORTUNA MALA

I tried sounding it out, but it wasn't ringing any bells.

What did all of this have to do with Val's *transformation*, as she described it? Nothing at all—a mere coincidence? Or everything? The longer I stared at the rock, the more certain I became that it was the latter. Holding it, tracing the etched pattern and letters with my thumb, feeling the contrast between the soft edges of the engraving and its smooth, flat backdrop, knowing instinctively that the stone was *old*, older than I could fathom...

Could it be that my tried and true beliefs in science and logic had failed me? That maybe, after all, something outside the realm of possibility was happening? The evidence, as it were, continued to mount up in favor of the weird, the otherworldly—and I was *so* close to accepting it—yet a part of me still resisted. I didn't think I'd ever tried so hard to ignore an answer that sat so readily in front of my face. *But*, I did know that denial wouldn't get me anywhere. I *had* to take that leap. I had to believe the stone held some meaning, the next step in figuring out what was going on and, hopefully, how I could reverse it.

I went for my bag to get my computer when my phone rang. The sound startled me. I laughed nervously, not realizing how spellbound I'd become with the stone and the raven iconography. It was an unknown number again. The same as before? I couldn't remember, but this time I answered.

"Hello?"

"Lindsay Hawkins?" asked a female voice.

"Yeah, speaking."

"This is Detective Sommers with the Grand Rapids Police Department. You're a difficult woman to reach, you know that, Ms. Hawkins?"

"Sorry, I've been staying at Val—a friend's." I wasn't sure why I said anything.

"Would that be Valerie Thompson?"

I sighed. "The one and only."

"You two are close, then."

"Yeah, sure. What does that matter?" I said it through clenched teeth, though my legs were jittery. I felt cold, but a thin sheen of sweat covered my skin.

"Easy there, I just wanted to ask you a couple questions. As someone close to Ms. Thompson, I assume you know that her boyfriend, Robert Wiggins, has been reported missing. Reported by Ms. Thompson, in fact."

"Yeah, Bobby. Of course I know."

"Care to tell me what else you know? Any information that might shed some light on Mr. Wiggins's disappearance?"

"Well what did Val tell you? That's all you need to know," I said before I could stop myself. It was a gut reaction from nerves, but also from a general dislike of police. Any organization with that much power was guilty in my eyes until proven otherwise.

"Perhaps you have some thoughts of your own?" Detective Sommers asked, politely, but with an edge to her voice. "How about you start by telling me about the day Mr. Wiggins went missing. Ms. Thompson said you two were together."

"Fine, yeah. We were. We met at Hidden Lake Preserve last Saturday morning to go for a walk like we do often. When we got done hiking, we decided to tool around town since it was so nice. And that's it."

"Whose car did you drive?"

"Excuse me?"

"I asked whose car. You said you met her there. I assume that means you drove separately. So, did you take your car or Ms. Thompson's to...*tool around town?*"

"Oh, um, well, mine. We took my car."

"How come?"

"How come? I don't know, why does it matter?"

"And you left Ms. Thompson's car at the preserve?"

"Sure, yeah."

"Is it sure or yeah?"

"Yes, we did. Okay? God, what is the deal?"

"Just trying to clarify details, Ms. Hawkins. Easy does it."

"Will you stop doing that?" I said. "Stop telling me to be calm. Jesus."

"I wouldn't *have* to tell you if you *were* calm. But you are awfully agitated. Is there something you'd like to share?"

I was about to reply something snarky, then paused. Did I want to share what really happened? I couldn't possibly want to do that, could I? Turn my best friend in and let Bobby win, like she said? But no, that wasn't right either. Bobby *couldn't win*. He was dead. That was what I told Val then, and it sure as hell was still true now. Fucking Bobby Wiggins, murdered in cold blood, and I was helping her get away with it. I always believed I was a ride or die type of friend, but how fair was it of Val to throw me into her shit and ask me to clean it up? What if she got caught and I had said nothing? I was no lawyer, but I'd seen enough stupid ass cop shows to know that made me a criminal, too. I had to ask myself the question: was this new version of Val worth the risk?

"Ms. Hawkins?" the detective said, snapping me out of my haze of reflection.

I cleared my throat and made my decision.

A life of always wondering, always worrying—more than usual—was not a life I wanted. And maybe, just maybe, Val could get the help she clearly needed.

I opened my mouth to spill my guts, but what came out was, "I'm fine. Are we done here?"

My jaw hung open as Detective Sommers said something I didn't hear. I was too busy marveling at the words that had emerged from my lips. I was prepared to confess, turn my best friend over to the law, but my brain, or *something*, wouldn't allow it.

I tried again, ignoring whatever Sommers was saying, preparing to say *Val killed Bobby*.

"I'm fine," I said again, and shook my head until I felt dizzy. *What the fuck is going on?*

"Ms. Hawkins?" I heard the Detective say finally.

"Sorry, what?"

"I said I had one more question. Did Ms. Thompson mention anything about Mr. Wiggins on your hike?"

"Oh. Sure, just that he stayed over the night before and left early Saturday morning."

"Nothing about where he went?"

"No," I responded, regaining my composure, but my mind still spun. Had I really attempted to confess and failed? What was I thinking? More importantly, why couldn't I?

"Nothing at all?"

"Look, I assume he went home. Or to work. I don't know. Val doesn't say much about Bobby to me because she knows I don't like him."

"Not a fan of Mr. Wiggins?"

"Of course not. He's an asshole. If you'd spent even a single minute with the guy you'd know it, too. You know, actually, if you do end up finding him? Do us all a favor and send him back to whatever hellhole he came from," I said, my sudden anger at remembering the type of man Bobby was reinvigorating my nerve, reaffirming my resolve to stand by Val. "And before you try to start something, Val knows what I think of Bobby already."

"I see. Well, thank you for your time, Ms. Hawkins. I'll be in touch if I have any more questions."

SEVENTEEN

I chugged one of the remaining two beers in the fridge and popped the top on the other before settling at the kitchen table with my computer and the engraved stone. Back to the matter at hand, and the only avenue left to take.

There was no point searching for things like *bird curse, raven curse, or bird raven curse,* because I'd exhausted that rudimentary and lazy course of action several times over by now. But now I had two additional pieces of information to work with: *FORTUNA MALA* and the stone in which the letters were etched.

A quick Google search told me *fortuna* had origins in ancient Roman culture, including the Goddess Fortuna, and that it roughly translated to: fortune, luck. The Goddess Fortuna was known to bring luck, good or bad. Bad being *mala.*

Bad Fortune.

Beside the fact that there was an image of a raven, the stone was starting to seem like it didn't have much to do with Val. Bad luck? According to her, she'd never been better, and I hadn't seen any misfortunes, just good news. Even the raven on this thing was alive and well, the opposite of every other one I'd seen since this whole thing started.

And yet, I couldn't shake the feeling that these words somehow awarded my curse theory some validation. The very existence of the stone was unsettling enough. But I wondered, why? Why the living raven with the bad fortune caption? It didn't make sense. A dead raven, now that would have made sense.

Back to Google, I tried *fortuna mala raven curse*. The results weren't good. The first couple pages were comprised mainly of random articles or scholarly works on the Goddess Fortuna, with the term *curse* being used in a more figurative way, and *raven* absent altogether. I tweaked the search a couple different ways, but ultimately came up empty.

Next, I tried Reddit, a site I loathed more than any other, yet frequented the most. It was like your favorite spite-follow on Facebook. You hated just about everything they posted, but you couldn't help lapping up every single word. Loving their idiocy, feeding off their ignorance, and seething in rage that you'll never release back on them. Reddit was like that, only a thousand times worse. Any information I could ever hope to find was there, right alongside the most heinous commentaries and the ugliest bottom-feeding trolls on the internet.

I went to the Occult subreddit and took my shot by searching *fortuna mala*, wanting to start simple and to avoid casting too narrow a net. A single result came back.

Help! My sister cursed by a bird. Fortuna Mala??

I choked on a mouthful of beer as I read the post title, coughing until my airway was clear enough to take another swig.

"What are the fucking chances?" I muttered.

It was posted almost two years earlier by someone with the username *AnonEmouse*—clever.

The post said:

Someone help please! My sister touched a dead bird and now she's...cursed I guess? She says she has changed. No—her "transfiguration." Says she has never been happier. She dropped out of college and quit her part time job. My parents are freaking out, but my sis doesnt care. Its not just that...I've seen her...do things. Bad things. It doesnt make sense or seem real...but does anyone know anything? Has anyone herd of anything like this??

The only comment was from a classic Redditor dickhead:

If she's happy why don't u leave her the fuck alone? Dum twat.

Two years and no help. Was this the poster's only hope? Had they found anything out? Where had their story ended? I clicked on AnonEmouse's user profile and started a private message, breaking my number one rule of never engaging another person on this clogged toilet of a site— but what choice did I have?

I wrote:

This is crazy, but I think my best friend has the same "curse" as your sister. She touched a dead bird. A big ass raven. And now she's different. She says everything she does is to create happiness, but...idk, she's bad, too. Did you ever figure it out? Please, can you tell me what happened??

I hit send, then leaned back in my chair. Responding felt necessary, right, and urgent, but now I had to wait. It was a hard thing for me to do. I sent my message out in a rush, so I wanted a response in kind. But really, who knew how long it would take? Who could say the person that made the post even used Reddit anymore, let alone had notifications or emails turned on?

I took a sip of beer, noticing that it was almost gone. Bummer, the last one. I wondered if Val had other booze in her cupboard, then thought about how this all started because I'd been searching for her secret weed stash which I never found. Then my mind, circling from thought to thought, settled on Val herself, and how she, my absolute best friend in the world, had implicitly *threatened me.*

A nasty thought turned my spit sour. What if AnonEmouse wasn't even alive anymore? What if they were dead, murdered by their cursed sister like Bobby? Or, possibly, me in the near future if Val found out what I'd been doing tonight—what I'd found.

Hell, maybe Val would kill me anyway. The moment I became too much of a drag on her happiness, I might as well kiss it all goodbye.

EIGHTEEN

I didn't hear from AnonEmouse that night or the next day. I did end up sticking around Val's apartment, hanging out with Patch, and, spurred on by boredom and an aching silence from my thread of Reddit hope, scoured every inch of that place looking for another clue.

I ended up eventually finding her weed, but by that point I was too much on a mission to care anymore. The baggy was in the vent like I thought, just pushed way back, like it was no longer needed.

Anyway, if Val found out I was snooping, she'd know I might've found something I wasn't supposed to. I made sure to clean everything up and return the stone. The last thing I wanted to do was create doubt in Val's mind and, consequently, spike my threat level.

By Sunday afternoon I'd finally left, remembering I had my own place to take care of, errands to run, groceries to get. While I was out and about, I got a text from Val saying she'd just landed and wondered if I wanted to meet up so she could blab about her trip and so on. I hesitated, but knew I couldn't avoid seeing her forever. Not unless I was prepared to leave her behind altogether.

Since I was already downtown, we agreed to meet for drinks at The Grand. Val said she was going to stop home first, so I opted to abandon my errands and show up early to snag a shot or two of whiskey before she arrived.

The bartender was chatty and cute, but I wasn't feeling up to small talk and had to keep asking him to repeat what he'd said. At one point I noticed him just staring at me and I realized he'd asked me a question.

"I'm sorry, I missed that?"

"I asked if you heard about that guy found dead in that alley a little while back?" he said.

"Oh, yeah, sure. What about him?"

"Well, they just released his name and picture. I shit you not I've met the guy before, and not that long ago either. He was in here with his girlfriend. They were a weird couple, seemed like things weren't going well for the guy. Wait, actually, it was his fiancé. Yeah, that's right, 'cause the news story I saw mentioned they were due to get married next month—"

"Damn," I said, without much sympathy, my mind elsewhere. "That's rough."

"It gets rougher. The chick had been found dead, too. Like right around the same time. Can you believe that shit? Washed up naked on the beach at—"

My phone chimed. New notification. Private message on Reddit from AnonEmouse.

"Sorry, got take this," I said without looking up. "Can I get another whiskey, though?"

The bartender shuffled away with a grumble and I read the message.

Idk why I'm bothering, I guess I'm just sick of it... Your trolling is neither funny nor original. Leave me alone, please.

I replied, "No troll. I'm serious. I need your help."

Prove it.

I thought for a second, thinking back to the original post and my message. What else could I say to prove I wasn't lying? Then I had it.

"I found a stone with the raven etched into it and the words FORTUNA MALA."

Was that the only stone?? Did you find the other one?

The only stone? What were they talking about? "Just the one. There's another?"

YES. You need the second stone to break the curse.

"Wait a minute. So there actually is a curse? I'm not... you know, crazy? And what about the two stones? What's on the other one? Idk, start from the beginning?"

The bartender placed the second shot of Jack in front of me and I knocked it back, immediately croaking at him for another. At the rate I was going, I'd be drunk before Val got there. But I didn't care. My only worry was finding out everything I needed to know about the curse before she arrived.

The curse is real. It's an old form of paganism.

"Like what, witches or some shit?"

Think Wiccans, but more evil.

"Okay. And there's TWO stones?"

There's the one you have, with the raven alive, mid-flight, the words FORTUNA MALA below—bad fortune. The other stone shows the raven dead, like you probably saw in real life, with the word FELICITAS—meaning happiness, more or less.

"And the stones break the curse?"

The stones are the key to all of it. And there are a few incantations you recite while holding a stone in each hand that do different things, all different parts of the curse. The first incantation calls forth a bird (like a crow or raven). The second one makes the bird drop dead, this is the sacrifice needed to set the curse. Then, while holding the two stones against the bird, you say the final short incantation—Faber est suae quisque fortunae. The next person to touch the bird is cursed.

I had so many questions. A random one popped to the front after rereading and seeing the second incantation made the bird drop dead.

"Do you think the stones could make a bunch of birds drop dead? All at once? We found a ton near the ritual site."

Bird kill, sure. It seems like that's a common side effect.

Bird kill. Yes, that's it. I shivered at the thought of this curse being the cause of mass bird death. The impossible power necessary for that. I thought back to all those unexplained instances I'd seen on the internet—could they be explained by this? Was one of those places where AnonEmouse lived?

It seemed likely.

I asked the next question on my mind. "Faber est suae quisque fortunae? What does that mean?"

Every man is the artisan of his own fortune.

"What's the point though? My friend calls it a gift, but it's clearly a curse. Right? At least for everyone else around her. What's the end game? And why the conflicting images and phrases?"

I call it Curse Corvus. Not sure if there's an actual name, but birds from the genus Corvus *seem to be at the root of it. Anyway, it's designed to infect strangers with a relentless desire to pursue happiness at all costs. An act of evil, as far as I'm concerned. The cursed ones think it a gift, taken from/given to them by the bird. The curse convinces them the sacrificed bird is their blessing, a stroke of good fortune maybe, but what they don't see is how it uses them to ruin everything around them.*

And eventually, themselves.

"Eventually themselves…how so?"

You asked what the end game is. That's it. A reckless pursuit of happiness with no caution for consequences can't go on forever. Eventually it catches up.

"Like what, the law or something?" I responded, thinking of Bobby and my recent conversation with Detective Sommers.

Possibly, but it's more personal than that, to the cursed one. This infection or disease or whatever you want to call it runs rampant in them, propelling them to rid their lives of every single negative thing, no matter how small. Eventually they come to the conclusion that there's nothing more they can do, they'll never be entirely free of negativity. The only option left is to take themselves out of the cosmic picture.

"They commit suicide?"

Yeah. But not before they reset the curse for another stranger. That's how it survives and perpetuates.

I sat back heavily. It was all too much. All absurd.

Yet, it made perfect sense. Happiness and bad luck. Happiness for Val, bad luck for everyone else...and if this AnonEmouse person was telling the truth, eventually bad luck for Val, too. I wanted to reject the prospect of this curse ending in Val's suicide, but suddenly a thought hit me like a bus. A possible connection made. The man in the dumpster and his fiancé, the woman found naked, drowned out in Lake Michigan...

A quick Google search on my phone brought up the news story on the couple's tragic ending. I scrolled through the article until I found a photo, shared with the news by a family member or friend no doubt: the dead woman, standing in a hipster-looking resale shop, flanked by a couple other women, utterly beaming with joy and holding—

A wedding dress. *The* fucking wedding dress. Holy shit, it all made sense now. She was the previously cursed one, and the dead guy, her soon-to-be husband, probably her victim. Perhaps her last before taking her own life.

And if that all was true, could I really not fathom a similar result for Val?

"How did you find all this out?"

You'd be surprised what you can find on the dark web.

I nodded to myself. I *would* be surprised, if I could ever actually find the damn dark web. I wanted to know more, but I was afraid details might get lost or muddled in translation across messages like this.

"Do you have a name? A phone number maybe to communicate easier?"

I'd rather not.

"Okay, sure. I understand." And while frustrated, I did understand. We were both strangers on the internet. Sometimes—most times—opening up in situations like that brought more harm than good.

"Then what about the cure or whatever? How does that work? I need to fix my friend before she kills herself."

It's simple. Hold the stones against the cursed person, then recite the incantation backwards—fortunae quisque suae est Faber.

I whispered the phrase several times, trying it out on my tongue. It rolled smoothly enough, considering it was Latin and I didn't speak a lick of it. I thought I could remember it if necessary.

"That's it?"

That's it.

Then I realized my mistake. "What if you only have one stone?"

Then it won't work. You need both.

"How am I supposed to find it? What if I can't?"

Well, if you can't, I'm sorry. There's nothing you can do. But I'm sure it's around. The stones must be left with the sacrificed bird for the curse to be passed along. They need the stones. My sister had both, so I'm guessing your friend does, too.

"Any reason she might keep them separate?"

I'm sure she is. I think they—the cursed ones—know they are important.

"Meaning?"

Well, I'm speculating a bit here, but I think the cursed ones know the stones are important, but I don't think they're aware why. I don't know if they have any idea the curse can be broken, but they must feel like someone else having the stones is a threat to them. The bottom line is they know nothing about the bad.

At least my sister didn't.

"I'm sorry, I never asked...how is your sister? Is she okay now?"

No.

I waited a minute for more, but that was all AnonEmouse sent. "Oh... I'm sorry. I thought you said the 'cure' worked? You know all this stuff... I thought you'd figured out how to fix it."

And the more I thought about it, the more I understood. She did figure out how to fix it, but it must have been too late. Her sister had already taken care of it.

Another message came through.

The cure works. You can break the curse. Find the other stone and follow the instructions.

I ordered a beer, already feeling on the wrong side— or good, depending on your perspective—of buzzed.

I read and reread all of AnonEmouse's messages. As impossible as it seemed, this had to be the real deal, right? Did I even have the option to ignore it anymore? No, I didn't think I could. I had to accept this as fact. I *had* to. Val was cursed and she was a threat—to me, to anyone else foolish or ignorant enough to stand in her way, and perhaps, most importantly, to herself. I couldn't let this continue, nor could I allow Val's story to end the same way as my mom's. I wasn't there to save my mom from herself, but I would not make the same mistake with Val.

My phone chimed. Another message from AnonEmouse.

There's something else you need to know. There's one more way the curse perpetuates—

"Hey Lindsay," Val said from behind me, and I almost screamed.

NINETEEN

I blurted a shrill, overenthusiastic "Hey!" back, then managed to thumb the display button on my phone and shove it into my pocket before she could see what was on my screen.

"*Finally,* someone happy to see me. I mean, for God's sake, what does a girl have to do?"

"Huh?"

"Patch being a dick, as usual," she said as she turned away, motioning to the bartender to order.

She got her drink, and we moved to an empty table— easy to do on a late-Spring Sunday evening, with only a smattering of diehard drunks and golf fans taking up space. Once settled, Val lifted her glass and instinctively, I did too. But she wasn't going for the glass tap, as was tradition, only a drink. I shouldn't have been surprised, but I was. Nothing was sacred.

I took a drink of my own, hoping my bitterness would wash away before I spoke. "So, how was—"

"Oh my God, you have to hear about my trip," Val said, interrupting the very question I was going to ask.

"Sure, let's hear it."

"So, the weather was gorgeous, which, I think it always is in San Diego, but still. And there's so much to do. Tons of shopping and great restaurants and breweries—all on company dime," she said, winking. "And the beaches are stunning. I really think I could live there. It's honestly not even as expensive as you'd think. I mean, it *is* Cali, but," she shrugged, "somewhat affordable."

"Sounds like you had a great trip," I said, because I didn't want her to hear what I really thought. And, I didn't want to hear it out loud either. I hated the murky jealousy rising in my chest, but didn't know how to stamp it down.

"Oh yeah, so cool."

"And what about the work part?"

"Huh? Oh, yeah, that was fine. It was pretty low-key. I went to a couple presentations, then, you know, just skipped the rest."

"Your employer won't care? I'm guessing it wasn't cheap to send you all the way out there. Won't they want a report or something, like proof you learned something?"

Val waved a hand, then took a noisy swig of beer. "Nah. If my boss asks for anything specific, I'll just make him understand that everything is fine."

She said it so nonchalantly, I wasn't sure I heard her correctly. "What does that mean? *Make him understand?*"

"Oh, you know."

"No, I don't know. What does it mean?"

"Lindsay, you know exactly what it means. I've done it to you, too," she replied airily, then, I swear to God, patted my arm in a bullshit patronizing way.

I pulled away. "Val, what—"

"Hey, how was your talk with Detective Sommers?"

"What? How did you know I talked to her?"

"I warned you she was going to get a hold of you, didn't I?"

"Right, yeah, it was fine. What you said it'd be."

"You didn't tattle on me, did you?"

"What? No, of course—"

"Come on, I'm only kidding. I know you can't tell anyone what happened. See, I told you you knew what I meant." She smiled at me brightly before taking a drink.

"What the fuck, Val. What did you do to me?"

"Keep your voice down, Linds. Sheesh, the golf douche in the back might hear you," Val said, laughing. "But for real, you're fine. Part of my gift is being able to convince people. I simply convinced you to not turn me in to the police. Or anyone, for that matter. And," she held up a hand, "before you start up again, I did it to *protect* you. And me, of course. I know you wouldn't betray me, but if for some reason you got a funny thought in your head when the police inevitably called… well, I prevented any-thing bad from happening, is all."

"I don't care *why* you did it; you shouldn't have. It's a real invasion of… privacy? I don't know. You violated me—my trust, at the very least. That shit is not okay."

She watched me, blandly, over the top of her glass. "Are you done?"

"Goddamnit, Val. Stop *doing* that. It's so annoying. And condescending."

"Lindsay, you need to calm down," she said, staring directly into my eyes.

And I did calm down. I couldn't do otherwise if I tried. A warmth flushed through me, setting my nerve endings a-tingle, and for a moment I forgot where I was or what I was doing, only that whatever worries I had were gone.

She watched me curiously, and I wondered about that, but I couldn't find the train of thought that had left the station, if there had ever been one.

Val leaned back, casually drained her beer, and called the bartender for another. I took a drink, too, trying to re-ground myself in my surroundings, trying to find my place in whatever I'd been doing here at the table with her. Slowly, the conversation came back to me, along with an itch in the back of my skull. I scratched it absently, but found it was under the bone, like a centipede had burrowed into my head through my ear canal and crawled its way around the back of my gray matter. The sensation was odd and unsettling, but not entirely unpleasant, either.

I waited for it to pass. In its wake was the realization that Val had done something to me. She'd done that *thing* to me again, forced me to do or think or act against my will, and while I wanted to be furious, wanted to stand and flip the table at the intrusion—at her audacity—I couldn't. A fresh wave of peace and relaxation flooded my body, and I could only be calm.

So, I couldn't be angry, but I was on guard now. This was the level she was playing at. We no longer existed on a two-way street. This was Val's one-way, and if I obstructed her flow, she'd force me to change.

The question now, though, was how much longer would she settle with *changing* me instead of resorting to more permanent measures?

I raised my eyes to her, who'd been at ease, letting me regroup.

"Feeling better?" she asked.

"I feel great," I replied, then tried on a smile. It felt faker than hell, but it seemed to work.

"As intended." She smiled back.

"But," I said, pausing to ponder my words, "for the sake of my sanity—no, *our friendship*, could you please try to understand how that could feel to me? That you think you know what's best for me, *and* that you're making me do things without asking me first?"

"But I *do* know what's best. I know the *true* path to happiness."

I closed my eyes, willing myself to remain calm—which was becoming more difficult and had me wondering what the reach of Val's *gifts* was. A problem for another day. When I opened my eyes, Val was staring at me, waiting. Further objection rested in my mouth, waiting to tumble out, but it would do no good. What if I pushed too hard?

"Yeah, okay, Val."

She stood suddenly. "I have to pee."

While she was gone, I sipped my beer and wondered just how thin the ice below my feet was. I zoned out for a second, then found myself staring at Val's purse, hanging on the back of her vacated chair.

It couldn't be. Could it?

I glanced at the bathroom door, considered how much time I might have, then quickly reached over and pulled her purse to me, rummaging through the million pockets as fast as humanly possible.

But the second stone wasn't there.

I dropped the purse back over the chair as the door to bathroom swung open and Val came sauntering back. I kept my eyes on her pockets, looking for the bulge or outline of the stone. I couldn't tell for sure, but she didn't appear to be carrying it with her. Not if it was the same size as the one I found, and I could only assume it was.

So, she didn't have it with her. But where? Had to be in her apartment, right? Or maybe she stuffed it away in a safety deposit box... I'd never get it if that were the case.

In her seat again, Val abruptly said, "Did you know San Diego had such a homelessness problem?"

"What? No, I guess I didn't."

"Terrible, really. The weather is nice all year round, so it's not surprising honestly. And easier to get to than Hawaii."

"I can see that. So... what's your—"

"I had a run-in with a homeless guy. The only negative experience of the whole trip, actually."

"Run-in? What, like he asked you for some money or food or something?"

"It started out that way. I was walking to get some lunch and this filthy guy hopped up from his perch by the 7-11 and started following me, asking me for money. I said no, obviously, and tried to ignore him, but he was a persistent bitch. He asked for food next and all I could think about was how he smelled of rank piss, and I wondered if I'd even have an appetite when I got where I was going. I said no again, but he kept coming. I was getting more than a little annoyed at this point, but figured eventually he'd fall back and leave me alone."

She paused to take a drink. I couldn't help but notice a glow in her eyes.

"Why are you telling me this?"

She held up a finger as she took another swallow, then said, "Well, the hobo had one more question for me. He asked for money again, but this time said he wanted it for booze. I'll admit, that got me to stop. Sure, he'd lied before, but I appreciated his honesty now. And believe it or not, I actually considered giving him money. I decided against it, though, not wanting to encourage bad behavior and all. So, I turned to him and tried to tell him to leave me alone. But he got to me before I could. He stepped closer and suddenly my nose was filled with not just stale piss, but actual rotting garbage. His breath stank. His entire *body* reeked of shit and piss and *rot*, and I *knew*, just knew I had to do something."

I cocked my head, confused. "Wait, so you did give him money then?"

Oh, my ignorance.

"God, no," she said, lowering her voice but still speaking forcefully—whisper shouting. "I ushered him to the nearest alley, pepper-sprayed him in the eyes, then told him to kill himself."

"You did what?"

"Now, admittedly, I wasn't sure if my reach went quite that far. Still trying to figure that out, to be honest, because apparently over the phone it doesn't work at all, which is bullshit. But anyway, the piece of shit surprised me. He grabbed a broken glass bottle off the ground and stabbed himself in the throat. My God, talk about full points for creativity."

"Holy shit," I said, propelled backward in my chair from the shock and immediate desire to be further away from Val. "No, Val, no… you didn't… you're kidding, right?"

"Why would I kid about that?"

"I honestly don't know. But why? You can't—Val, no…"

"What did he have to live for, anyway?"

I didn't move—couldn't move. My mouth opened and closed noiselessly, like a fish out of water, wanting to say something but at the same time… what the fuck could I say to that?

Val could not be bothered. She scrolled through social media on her phone, as if all she'd shared was a passing comment about the weather and not that horrifically disturbing story. Finally, my mouth opened and words came out.

"I have to go."

She looked up, surprised. "So soon?"

"Yeah, sorry, forgot I wanted to finish up a job app tonight."

"Still no luck, huh?" she asked as I stood, scrounging in my pockets for money. Thankfully, I had cash on hand so I could drop some bills and leave.

"No luck. Hopefully soon, though." I turned to go. "Catch you later."

I got a full step away when Val called my name. I glanced back over my shoulder.

"Got my spare key?"

I turned away for a moment, processing and planning. I'd heard her question, but I stalled, a sudden feeling told me my response was crucial to what I had to do next. "I'm sorry, what?"

"My key. Do you have it?"

And I had it—the idea. "Oh, shit, I'm sorry," I said, smacking my thigh. "I'm such an idiot. I left it at my place on my table. Meant to grab it as I walked out." I shook my head, playing up my self-disgust.

"Linds, it's fine. I'll get it from you later."

"Okay. You sure? You could come by now, or are you staying for more drinks?" I asked, trying to remain casual, hoping she didn't hear the strain in my voice.

"Eh, I might knock back another. Not much longer, though. Still have to unpack and get ready for work tomorrow."

I nodded, then waved and forced a calm, if stilted, walk to the door. The second I got outside, I sprinted to my car. I had work to do, and not much time to do it.

I had an apartment to toss.

TWENTY

I raced to Val's apartment, unsure whether I had a couple minutes or an hour to search the place. I had her key—which had been in my pocket—out and my seatbelt off before my car came to a stop in the parking lot. I vaulted out and to the door, then made my way to her apartment.

The door slammed behind me, but I paid it no mind as I scanned the main room, catching my breath. I'd practically turned the apartment upside down while she was out in San Diego, so I didn't know what I expected to find this time around. Still, if AnonEmouse was right—and if *I* was right about Val not having it on her—she had the second stone *somewhere*, and her apartment was the only place that made sense.

I swung my gaze side to side, deciding where to begin. I didn't want to simply toss shit everywhere, but to be somewhat methodical. As I looked, a sour note struck in my head, but I couldn't immediately place its source.

Something about Val's apartment seemed off, but I didn't have time to worry about it now.

My gaze settled on the vent where I found the first stone. That was as good a place to start as any. If I was going to do what had to be done, I needed both stones. Might as well get that one first.

I yanked the vent off the wall and jabbed my hand into the hole, swatting around until my fingers brushed the smooth surface of the stone. I pulled it free, then made another sweep just in case I'd somehow missed something before. As expected—only weed.

I shoved the vent back into place and jumped to my feet, the first stone in my back pocket. I checked the time and saw a few minutes had passed already. I could be out of time. Val could be home any second if I was unlucky.

FORTUNA MALA flashed so bright in my mind's eye I could almost feel heat from the stone on my ass.

Scrambling, I thought again of likely hiding places and ran to the bathroom off Val's room, checking behind the toilet tank, and even inside the tank, but nothing. The nightstand next to her bed also came up empty. Again, I'd checked all these places before, how would they be different—

Yes, different. What *was* different now? Well, Val was back from her trip, that was different. I came back to the earlier thought of Val keeping the stone on her. That still didn't help me right now, but—

But, what if she had it *with* her, not necessarily *on* her. Like, for example, in her—

Luggage.

From Val's room I made my way toward the entry where I'd seen her suitcase propped upright next to the kitchen table. As I passed the guest bathroom, I suddenly stopped, realizing what had caused the *off* feeling I'd had before.

Patch.

He hadn't greeted me when I came through the door, hadn't shown his face since I'd been here. I stepped into the bathroom and flipped the light switch. I took the two steps to the tub where Val kept his litter box and pulled the shower curtain back, already knowing what I'd find, but still hoping.

I gasped anyway.

Patch on his side in the litter box, eyes wide and staring, body unmoving. His beautiful calico fur matted and ruined with blood.

I yanked the curtain back, trying to shield myself from the dead cat, nearly ripping the curtain off the rod. I staggered out of the bathroom, crying, moving with subconscious intention to Val's suitcase, *needing* to end this.

The outer pocket zipper got stuck partway and needed careful removal from the caught fabric, wasting more time I didn't have, exacerbating my already inflated frustrations. Worse, when I got it open and rummaged through, I found nothing. The main compartment was next. It came easily—thank God—after which I lifted the suitcase and gave it shake. A cascade of clothes fell out, followed by a dull *thunk* against the linoleum floor.

Bingo.

There, nestled in one of Val's tops, was the second stone. Lifting it to my face, I saw what was etched on its surface. The engraved image of a dead raven was as close to identical to Val's tattoo as I could remember. Below the bird was the word *FELICITAS*.

This was it, her *happiness* stone.

I stood, pulling the first stone from my pocket, and held the two side by side. In one hand, the contrasting images of a lively, in-flight raven with the caption of *bad fortune*; in the other, a dead raven and *happiness*. Together, they created a world of shit for me, my best friend, and anyone who dared cross her.

I spared a glance at the time. I'd been there nearly fifteen minutes. I didn't have much longer.

I crossed the living room area and peeked out the windows at the parking lot. Val's car was bouncing over the last speed bump on the drive outside her building. There was a chance she hadn't seen my car, but that was unlikely—I'd parked as close to the sidewalk of the building as possible. But that didn't matter now. She'd know soon enough I was here. I just had to get out and to my car before she could stop me.

I pocketed the two stones and leaped three strides back to the door, ripped it open, then sprinted down the hallway away from the main stairwell. There was another set of stairs at the back of the building, which led down to an exit further from my car, but no problem. I figured by the time I ran around the building back to the parking lot, Val would be parked and headed up.

The rubber from my tires would be meeting the road before she knew what happened.

TWENTY-ONE

I didn't know where I was driving until I was already on the way; my hands and feet clearly in on the plan from the get-go, while my brain took a beat to get it in gear and catch up. I figured it out by the time Val called.

"Lindsay," she said, her low, gritted-teeth voice sounding tinny and less menacing than I'm sure she meant it over my car's speakers. "Where are my stones?"

"With me."

"You have no idea what you're doing. What could you possibly know?"

"Enough."

"Lindsay, where are you going? You need to bring back my stones."

"No, I don't think I will. Your little trick doesn't work remotely, remember? I'm going to the Lake, and I'm going to make sure no one ever finds these stones again. End it where it started, you know? Because I'm sick of your shit, Val. You wanna stop me? Come fucking try."

"Getting rid of them won't stop me. I don't *need* them," Val snarled.

"Then why do you care so much?"

Silence. Then, "LINDS—"

I hung up.

I continued west, toward the lakeshore. It was obvious I was playing a little too fast and loose with my plan, but I was determined to make it work. I had every intention of chucking both stones into the depths of Lake Michigan, but not before I broke Val's curse. Not before I saved my best friend.

The more I thought about it, the more it seemed Val was unaware that the curse could be broken. Or perhaps she assumed I was too ignorant about the details of *her gift* to know better. Either way, I knew I had given her enough of a tug to follow me out to Rosy Mound Natural Area where, hopefully, I could surprise her, break the curse, and rid our lives of the stones, lest she be tempted to give it another shot. Whether she would be furious with me after, or forever indebted to me for saving her, I didn't know. I gave it fifty-fifty odds. It didn't matter now. I'd deal with it when the time came.

When I pulled into the empty parking lot, the bottom rim of the sun was nestled into the treetops. There'd be more sunlight past the trees and out in the dunes, and I estimated there to be somewhere between an hour and two before sunset. Plenty of time for what I had planned, as long as Val held up her end—and I knew she would.

I grabbed my bag, hopped from the car, and, with the stones in my pocket, jogged down the main forest trail. When I reached the break in the trees I was out of breath, had a stitch in my midsection, and could feel the liquor and beer roiling with the acid in my stomach. Add the mounting stress of the situation, and my body needed to eject some of its liquid cargo. I didn't have a say in the matter. I came to a sudden, lurching stop on the dune boardwalk, leaned to my left, and vomited into the sand. Unfortunately, I misjudged the wind and managed to blow bile into the strands of hair hanging around my face, and even got a little on my shirt.

"*Fuck*," I growled between gagging and spitting. I wiped at my mouth with my sleeve, then pressed on.

Halfway to the shoreline, I came to the first overlook and a set of stairs along the side that led down to a lower boardwalk and, subsequently, to another lookout point before continuing down to the water.

I stopped at the overlook, peering down at the landscape in front of me, trying to envision the scenario I had planned. Would it work? I had to count on a lot of luck, but I thought it might. Thankfully there was only one, looping path down to the water, and assuming Val would use the main parking lot—and see my car—she'd have to come the same way I did.

Taking the stairs two at a time, I rushed down to the lower boardwalk and ran to the second overlook. I dropped my bag on the platform there, then looked back at the first lookout to make sure the view still seemed right. I performed another mental run-through, then nodded, satisfied enough. It looked woefully like an obvious trap, my bag just sitting there out in the open, but I had to count on her anger and, more importantly, her brazen self-confidence, to take the bait. I had to trust my gut that she'd think she only needed to find me to succeed.

I jogged back to the base of the stairs, then carefully stepped off the boardwalk into the dune sand, taking a few delicate and deliberate steps up under the first lookout platform and back behind the stairs. I crouched down, pulling the stones out, one in each palm, facing out toward the water, toward where Val would emerge into view at the base of the stairs.

In position.

Several minutes passed. My calves and thighs burned, a true testament to my out-of-shapeness. My stomach felt empty and ached, and my breath reeked of rotten booze. Yet I remained, reciting the curse-breaking phrase, *fortunae quisque suae est faber*, over and over under my breath while I stared at the descending sun and listened for signs of Val's approach, like some torturous, anti-meditative trance.

Another minute passed. I had to stop reciting the Latin phrase, afraid if I said it too much, it would dissolve into more meaningless rubbish than it already was in my head and I'd end up saying it wrong when it really mattered.

The light breeze fluttered through the sprouting blades of dune grass. The wind was diminishing as the sunset deepened, the first red and orange hues blossoming on the horizon. That evening along the lake couldn't have been more pleasant and peaceful, and it had me wondering if that beautiful place was where I would die.

I felt hopeful that it was a sign of good things to come, but the moment was brief, flushed away by the memory of walking through Hidden Lake Preserve on that beautiful morning, to find Bobby soaking in his own blood. The movies had it wrong. Not all horror happens in the dark. In real life, it happened whenever it damn well pleased.

Thinking of unhappy endings reminded me of AnonEmouse's sister. A tight gasp exploded from my mouth as I remembered I never finished reading the messages. Was it a simple sendoff, or a warning I needed to heed?

I placed the *happiness* stone down gently in the sand, shifted to grab for my phone, and—

A noise, muffled by the miles of sand. But I knew what it was. A voice. Val's voice, calling my name.

I picked up the stone quickly, repositioned into my crouch. The muscles on both legs tensed, coiled tight like a spring, and I hoped they would allow themselves to be sprung, rather than cramp up when I needed to make my move.

"Lindsay!" Val called, closer, but still a ways back. I cocked my head slightly, listening for the soles of her shoes slapping against the wood planks, the sound gradually amplifying until it was right above me.

Val stopped. She *was* right above, standing on the platform of the lookout overhead.

"There you are," she whispered.

I almost released a groan, thinking she'd spotted me in my hiding spot, but at the last second clamped my lips shut. She'd only seen my bag, just like I planned.

She descended the steps. She was *so* close to me, and I prayed she wouldn't catch a whiff of the vomit stuck to my clothes, the cloying, acid aroma that seemed to suddenly fill the atmosphere. She reached the bottom and took two more steps, paused, then continued walking.

It was now or never.

I stood. Then, trying to match her cadence so her board-smacking could cover any of my own noise, I stepped when she stepped, staying in the sand and taking larger than normal strides to cover the distance between us.

Val came to a stop suddenly.

Time to act.

"*Fortunae quisque suae est faber*," I yelled as I strode once, twice, then leaped onto the boardwalk at Val. She reacted slowly, barely revolving a quarter turn before I finished the last syllable. A split second later, my hands, palm and stone first, slammed into her back. The impact rocked her forward, but she kept her feet.

I pulled back as she shrieked. Was that it? Had it worked?

She turned fully to face me. I'd never seen so many of her teeth at once; her face contorted somewhere between grinning and snarling. I could tell at once that I had failed to break the curse. She hadn't shrieked as a result of pain or some witch magic, nor was it out of terror.

Val shrieked out of pure bloodlust.

At the exact moment she said, "I'm going to kill you," I realized my mistake. I did it backwards. I recited the phrase first, then touched the stones to Val second.

"Oh shit."

Val launched at me and I braced myself.

I got my arms up to cover my face as she tackled me, sending us both tumbling to the boardwalk. I cried out as my ribs connected with the solid wood plank. Then a second time as one of Val's hands made it through my blocking arms, something cutting, tearing skin off my cheek. At first I thought it was her nails, that she'd clawed at my face like a wild animal, until I saw the knife in her hand, its blade glowing a purplish-pink from the sunset as she pulled back to strike again.

I shoved out at her, risking a slash to my exposed forearms. The move was enough to deflect her aim and allow me a chance to wrap my arms around her shoulders and roll us both off the boardwalk onto the sand, getting me on top of her now.

I think I surprised her, taking us into the sand, because she paused, her knife-wielding hand retracted by her face. I was amazed to find I still had both stones clutched in my hands.

For another second, we observed one another. Or maybe it was instant; a flash slowed down amid chaos, time experienced without regard to logical human construct. However long the moment lasted, I witnessed the wild, rampant fury in her eyes, her mouth bared, shrieking the war cry of the raven. I wondered what she saw in mine. I wanted to believe defensiveness and fear, but I wasn't sure that'd be accurate.

We both swung at the same time.

Val's knife buried into my side as the stone in my right hand, the *happiness* stone, crunched her orbital bone. Her avian screech morphed to a human wail, matched by my own screaming. I'd never felt such acute, intense pain before in my life. Yet it quickly dulled in the presence of my adrenaline igniting like jet fuel.

Again, we acted simultaneously, but Val's mistake was thinking she had time to protect her face. I didn't bother dealing with the knife in my side. Instead, I struck again.

Then again—left hand this time.

And right again.

My limbs moved independently of my consciousness now, as if controlled by an external force fueled by rage, frustration, and sorrow. I became dimly aware that I was speaking. Chanting, more like. "Please stop fighting, please stop fighting, pleasestopfighting..."

Left side. Smash.

Right side. Splat.

Val had stopped fighting a while ago.

Val had stopped everything a while ago.

Her head, now a muddled mess of ragged, bloody flesh and white chips of ivory bone, in no way supported breathing. Her right eye bludgeoned, buried, covered—gone. Her left eye not much more than a slit, but the pupil remained visible, staring at me.

I hovered over her, my hands—still holding the stones—planted in the sand on either side of her, my arms shaking, threatening to give out. My body shook violently, gasping for air, heaving with my sobs.

Tears dropped from my eyes to hers.

At some point I realized I was no longer above Val but lying beside her. The sky looked too dark. Yet, despite the seed of worry, I lazily turned my face to the horizon, refusing to move. The top edge of the sun was down to a point above the waterline.

I sat up, slowly, blinking. My body acted as if my alarm had just gone off too early to hop energetically out of bed.

Clumsily, I stood, feeling a pinch at my side. Moving at dial-up internet speeds, my eyes told my brain there was still a knife sticking out of me.

It burned like hell when I grasped the handle, but I yanked anyway.

I screamed bloody murder, scaring a nearby bird—a raven, from the looks of it—into flight.

That got things moving. My surroundings sped up, sounds became more rounded, colors more distinct. It was like one of those scenes in a war movie where the character was in the blast radius of a grenade or large explosion and everything moved slowly and out of focus until suddenly it all hit in real time again.

And now that things were moving, the knife wound on my side exploded with fiery pain, and my shirt and pants quickly became tacky with blood.

I pulled off my shirt and tied it around my waist, applying as much pressure on the wound as possible, grinding my teeth against the pain. It wasn't great, but it would have to do.

Then I got to work.

The hardest, most exhausting part *physically* was moving Val's body up and down the rest of the dunes. I had to half-carry, half-drag her across the beach and as far as I could into the ice-cold waters of Lake Michigan, with rocks for extra weight.

But not *those* rocks. The cursed stones—the murder weapons—were thrown as far as my tired arm could get them in opposite directions.

The most difficult part *emotionally* was seeing the ruined mess of Val's face again. I left it exposed at first, but when I started to drag her by the armpits—her smashed watermelon of a head too close to my own—my body revolted. Convulsions of dry heaves tried to empty my already hollow pit of a stomach. After that, I pulled her shirt up over her head. Doing so exposed her massive raven tattoo in its entirety—turned out I was right about the bundle of sheets tattooed at the bird's feet. The sight was one I could have gone the rest of my life without seeing, but it was far better than what was left of her face.

The most tedious part was retracing every step, at first by twilight, then eventually by phone flashlight, kicking sand and covering up as much evidence of my being there as possible. At the site of our fight, where the majority of the blood had been spilled, I had to do a fair amount of digging to come close to erasing our trace.

Eventually I'd done what I could, resigned to whatever fate awaited me. I retrieved my bag and trudged back up the boardwalk by meager moonlight and stumbled through the trees in near perfect darkness, my hair and clothes still soaked with a mixture of lake water and blood.

I must have made it to my car, must have found my way home, because I woke up in my bed the next day at noon. I didn't leave my apartment again for several days, barely left my bed in all that time. My world spiraled into a manic haze. My body, mind, and spirit felt on the verge of death. I welcomed it.

But the haze passed. Whatever happened within the haze also passed. Five days came and went before I emerged on the other side.

And I'd never felt better in my life.

TWENTY-TWO

I t took two weeks for Val's body to wash up on shore.

By then, the lake had done a number on her. There was talk of suicide, but ultimately the police ruled it an accidental drowning. Val's family, confused and angry about the inexplicably extreme condition of her head, pushed hard enough to get the investigation reopened. I wasn't worried, though.

Detective Sommers came to see me. Said she had some questions about Val's death. She also mentioned, with a wry smile, that a patron of Hidden Lake Preserve found Bobby's body.

Giving the detective the eye contact she no doubt sought, I told her I had nothing to do with either death, and that she had no more questions for me. It seemed I was awfully persuasive these days, because she left with an apology and a good riddance.

Had I seen the rest of AnonEmouse's messages in time, I would have known that suicide was only one of two methods for spreading the curse. The second occurred when the cursed one was killed. In death, the cursed one relinquished their burden to the person responsible.

I wondered about that, most. What would have been different if I had known that before my final confrontation with Val? I could hope things would have gone differently, but I didn't know that they would have.

Honestly, I was surprised to feel any sort of remorse or guilt after realizing what happened to me, especially considering how Val acted all along. *Had* she felt anything lingering from 'before', like me? It didn't seem like it. Maybe the difference was how the curse was passed. Maybe my prior knowledge of the curse afforded me another chance.

I recently started taking scuba diving lessons, though.

It really was weird, knowing I needed to retrieve the stones to break my own curse. I often thought about other cursed ones like me—aware of their own fate—and how they'd fared. There had to have been others who'd known. But how did their stories end?

Some days I felt confident, remembering the curse's true intention, knowing how bad it got. Then, there were the days that I had trouble recalling my time before, days when I had trouble remembering the face of my former best friend. Days when I could remember that I need to recover the stones from Lake Michigan… but could not remember why—only that they were important to my story.

Some days, I dreamt of the cool water's undulating embrace, wondering just how deep I could go.

ACKNOWLEDGMENTS

We all know books don't happen without help, right? Well, I certainly had plenty, and I owe those folks lots of thanks.

First off, thanks to my sister, Lydia, and her best friend, Victoria. This book is dedicated to them, and rightly so. Much of what happens in the opening chapter happened in real life to them. The wedding dress and the bundled-up bird in the dunes along Lake Michigan...yep, true story. Everything else is fictious, but without their experience and photos, this book doesn't exist. Thanks again for letting me steal your story, L & V.

Secondly, I want to thank my family. To my wife, Korie, for the constant support, even if a lot of it is just accepting that my nights will mostly be spent toiled away in my office, working on this whole writer thing. Your love is all I need. And to Mom, Dad, and Sandi, for unending encouragement, and for being my first first readers.

Thanks to the "Minicrew/coven": Alexis DuBon, Brandon Applegate, Dan Bjork, and Eric Raglin. Y'all make my days better, and I wouldn't be the writer (or person) I am without you.

Extra thanks to Alexis for being such a great beta-buddy on this book (and all other times). Thanks to Darla Davis and Keith LaFountaine for early beta-reads, too.

To Alex Woodroe, for the brilliant edits, coaching, and invaluable publishing advice. And for being a friend.

Lastly, with regards to the book and its appearance, a massive thanks to both Evangeline Gallagher for gracing the cover with the perfect art, and Christopher Castillo Díaz for stunning interior illustrations.

Just kidding—my final thanks, dear reader, I give to you. I wrote the book and read it far too many times, but it's in your hands now. As it should be.

ABOUT THE AUTHOR

Alex Ebenstein is a lifelong Michigander, where he lives with his wife, son, and dog. His daytime mapmaking career supports his nighttime addiction of writing horror and other speculative fiction. His debut horror novella, *Curse Corvus*, was released in April 2023, and his follow-up novella, *Melon Head Mayhem*, was released by Shortwave Publishing in July 2023. He is also the editor of the SPLIT SCREAM series, published by Tenebrous Press. Connect with him on social media @AlexEbenstein and keep up with writing news at alexebenstein.com.

CONTENT WARNINGS

Curse Corvus contains scenes that deal with:
*Suicide
*Animal death

Please be advised.